THE SERIAL STOWAWAY

Comments about the Writing of Robert Fromberg

How to Walk with Steve

"Fromberg has a remarkable ability to inject meaning into silence, into the cracks between sections, into all the things that remain unsaid."

—Brett Biebel, author of *48 Blitz*

"In refusing easy consolations, Fromberg has created a memoir that shines like polished bone."

—Patricia Eakins, author of
The Hungry Girls and Other Stories

"Never have I read a more authentic, deeply felt rendering of a child's developing mind.
—Leslie Lawrence, author of *The Death of Fred Astaire*

Gee, That Was Fun: 7 Days of Mayhem, 1983

"With uncanny wit and a pointillist painter's eye for detail, *Gee, That Was Fun* reminds us that the fabric of our lives and the trajectory of our country, for good or ill, are composed of the smaller moments: the daily decisions made and not made, the tiny revelations, the ordinary failures and triumphs."

—C. Matthew Smith, author of *Twentymile*

"You'll read Robert Fromberg's *Gee, That Was Fun* with a continuously mounting delight at what he is pulling off. [Y]ou're in Fromberg's world now…where you'll find the profound amid the quotidian, as long as you know where to look. Just don't have the patty melt."

—Justin Bryant, author of *Thunder from a Clear Blue Sky*

"[A] critical read delivered with such crooked charm one cannot help but be seduced."

—Cathleen Allyn Conway, author of *Bloofer*

"Robert Fromberg has written a unique and deeply meaningful work of fiction that scrutinizes the random punishments meted out by the universe."

—Christian Livermore, author of *The Very Special Dead*

Friends and Fiends, Pulp Stars and Pop Stars

"Fromberg possesses rare chronic patience—which, in turn, enables him to be an ultimate observer. In this collection of dissecting essays, we're reminded of how masterfully he can transpose his perceptions into essential commentary, at once able to welcome and scrutinize minutiae any lesser writer would overlook entirely."

—Gabriel Hart, author of *On High at Red Tide*

THE
SERIAL
STOWAWAY

ROBERT FROMBERG

INSPIRED BY A TRUE STORY

The Serial Stowaway

Copyright © 2025 Robert Fromberg

Although inspired by a true story, this is a work of fiction. All characters, names, and details are a product of the author's imagination. Any resemblance to actual persons, living or dead, is purely coincidental.

Cover design and illustration by Claire Stamler-Goody

ISBN: 979-8-89424-005-3

Portions of this book previously appeared in the journals *100subtexts* and *soanyway*.

Published by:
Trunk of My Car Cooperative
Kailua, Hawaii

For Sheryl

.

"What truth can I tell that's as good as this lie they believe?"

—Elaine May

CONTENTS

Chapter 1:
The Serial Stowaway
and the Shrugging Scholar

Preparing for her seventeenth airplane trip without a ticket, The Serial Stowaway stood to one side of the entrance to security checkpoint four, indicated in Chicago's O'Hare Airport by a startlingly saturated yellow sign high in the air, seemingly poised to crash onto those below at any moment. Hitching her nearly empty canvas tote bag further up her shoulder, The Serial Stowaway waited until she saw a stylish couple in their forties accompanied by a far less stylish man in his seventies, the man clearly as apprehensive about tagging along with his son and daughter-in-law (or perhaps his daughter and son-in-law) as they felt burdened to have their perhaps-newly-widowed father/father-in-law with them.

The Serial Stowaway glided in their direction, followed directly behind them as they joined the line, and as they neared the TSA checkpoint, practically nestled into the armpit of the presumed widower. She knew that she would register with the stylish couple even less palpably than did their father/ father-in-law, even when, impatience already leaking into their voices at this early stage of the trip, they asked their father/father-in-law if he had his driver's license and boarding pass ready. The Serial Stowaway also was sure that the widower would not object to a slim woman approaching his age with her gray hair in a self-executed mom-bob staking a claim to proximity closer than his daughter and son-in-law (or son and daughter-in-law).

Inevitably, the couple, and their father/father-in-law, followed by The Serial Stowaway, reached the first position in line and, before the next available transportation security administration agent could wave his hand in invitation, broke free of the line and headed toward the agent with more bumping and nudging of the father/father-in-law than any objective observer would deem necessary. At the agent's kiosk, the couple both attempted to direct the father/father-in-law's placement of his boarding pass onto the scanning screen, the confusion causing the pass to escape the grasps of all three and float downward in a series of elegant arcs. As the pass neared floor level, it assumed the trajectory of a crop-duster and glided past the security kiosk.

Unified in their desire to retrieve the boarding pass, but not coordinated in their tactics to do so, the son and daughter-in-law (or daughter and son-in-law) leaned toward one another, knocking skulls. As they grimaced more in exasperation than pain, their father/father-in-law, with a skillful

deep-knee bend, the product of an active calisthenics practice, dropped to the height of his gliding boarding pass. Retrieving the pass, however, would have required knocking the
legs out from under his daughter and son-in-law (or son and
daughter-in-law), who, while rubbing their heads, glaring at
one another, and formulating the accusations they would
later that day direct at one another, had their father/father-
in-law effectively trapped.

In the confusion, The Serial Stowaway, with only a skosh
less grace than the father/father-in-law, dropped into a
crouch of her own and duckwalked past the security kiosk.

She had planned, insofar as an unexpected event lasting
a split-second allows planning, to keep going, that of course
being the wisest means of getting past security unmolested,
but the boarding pass was so close, had in fact paused in mid-
air as if waiting for her. The Serial Stowaway reached out a
slender arm and snared it.

Still on her haunches at floor level, she glanced back and
saw, also on his haunches, the father/father-in-law, whose
eyes, through a gap in the forest of legs, met those of The
Serial Stowaway. He shrugged. The Serial Stowaway extended an arm through two unmatched knees, placing the
boarding pass into its owner's hand. She turned, performed
three more duckwalk steps, then rose, hitched up her canvas
tote, and lost herself in one of the lines leading toward the
baggage-scan conveyor belt.

Through security and into the concourse, after twenty-
odd minutes of assessment, The Serial Stowaway settled on a
gate at which a sufficient but not overwhelming cluster of

people was merging into a line in response to the words "now boarding all seats, all rows to Phoenix Sky Harbor Airport."

Rather than join the line, The Serial Stowaway drifted to the side of the post at which the gate attendant was scanning boarding passes and, to those who passed her scrutiny and scanning device, wishing a good flight as they disappeared into the maw of the gangway.

The Serial Stowaway's position was important. She needed to be near enough to the attendant to monitor activities, but far enough away to not appear to be poised to board the plane. Her gaze needed to appear fixed at some distant point as though this flight were no part of her thoughts. In short, she needed to be invisible.

At the same time, The Serial Stowaway studied the face of the gate attendant. To The Serial Stowaway, the attendant's face looked remarkably soft, like the world's most luxurious pillow. Each time the attendant wished a good flight to admitted passengers, she seemed to be sharing wisdom sad and grave, kind and conclusive.

With perhaps fifteen people still in line and one poised to hand over a boarding pass, the attendant's face froze, seeming to consider some large and newly encountered truth. She slowly raised her gaze toward the ceiling, as if to add fuel to her wisdom from a higher power. As the attendant closed her eyes, The Serial Stowaway slid past and into the gangway. As she did, she heard behind her the sound of the gate attendant's sneeze.

On the aircraft, The Serial Stowaway made her way to the rear and entered the restroom to the left of the aisle. When she sensed that most stragglers had found their assigned places, she emerged, evaluated the smattering of empty seats, and started forward.

At row twenty-one, The Serial Stowaway touched the shoulder of a tweed sport jacket worn by the man in the aisle seat to her left. When he looked up, she looked him in the eye, smiled, and pointed to the empty middle seat, on the other side of which was a person ensconced in sweat clothes, bulky headphones, and a sizable handheld video screen. The sport coat-clad man smiled back, shrugged, unfolded himself from his seat, and standing not quite erect as if concerned he would hit his head on the ceiling of the aircraft, stepped aside.

Seated, The Serial Stowaway drew the straps of her limp canvas bag down her arm and leaned forward to place the bag under the seat in front of her. She emerged just in time to see the nearly gaunt man beside her finish writing something with a ball-point pen in a top-bound spiral notebook, click to retract the pen's point, close the notebook with what might have been a touch of the theatrical, and return pen and notebook to the inner breast pocket of his sport jacket.

The Serial Stowaway was surprised that the notebook, which had not seemed particularly small, fit in the jacket pocket without the man having to jockey it into position.

A movement, expected but unwelcome, began. It was a single movement above the fluttering of many movements by passenger heads and shoulders seen above and around the seatbacks. A flight attendant, a woman as solid as The Serial Stowaway's seatmate was gaunt, paper in one hand and pen in the other, was walking down the aisle, the pace of her steps not unlike a bride and escort making their way toward the altar, but in this case metered by the attendant's glances to the left side of a row and to her paper, to the right side of a row and to her paper, row after row, each row bringing the flight attendant closer to The Serial Stowaway in row twenty-one.

To some extent, perhaps a significant extent, being invisible was inherent for, rather than performed by, The Serial Stowaway. In most situations, The Serial Stowaway's age, gender, ethnicity, and size removed her from the concern of people encountered routinely during the rounds of life. However, in a moment when she was being scrutinized, when the appropriateness of her presence, the rectitude of her character, and the lawfulness of her behavior were being assessed by one in a position to either limit her freedom or ignore any tug of suspicion, a specific effort toward invisibility was required.

How to describe this effort? Here, as is so often the case when trying to capture life's elusions and elations, language becomes, if not our enemy, a clumsy tool. As lame as phrases such as "I don't know what to say" or "I'm speechless" are when composing a thank-you note, forcing the verbal on a nonverbal experience can seem to disrespect that experience. However, this problem is a problem not for The Serial Stowaway, but only for the writers of the newspaper articles and books presuming to describe her adventures.

Becoming invisible, for The Serial Stowaway, is a kind of emptying that is also a kind of filling. It is as if she were an old-fashioned inflatable raft with not one but two valves, one mounted on either side of the raft's length. As is traditionally the case, when the valve at one end is opened, air eagerly begins to escape. However, if just after opening the valve at one end, the valve at the other end is opened, something enters the raft at a velocity equal to the escaping air. The air that leaves is the air that has been living within the raft, air that is functional but faintly stale. The something else that enters serves the same function as the air previously within: It allows the raft to hold its shape, to pass for an ordinary raft. Yet what enters the raft is not like the escaping air. It is not air, fresh or otherwise. It is the absence of air. As powerful as the potential energy of trapped air, it is the strength of no strength, the kineticism of stillness.

This emptying and filling are not sequential. The substance leaving is not replaced by the substance entering. Rather, emptying and filling exist in a balance—a balance sought but never fully achieved, a balance sensed the way one senses a wonderful event that may come any day now, a wonderful event the imminence of which is more wonderful than the event itself.

What being invisible is not, for The Serial Stowaway, is flawless. She knows that each instance involves reaching toward something tricky and hard to grasp, the achievement of which is based not on the intensity or sincerity of effort but on forces impossible to identify and beyond her control. Oh, she is always able to achieve some degree of invisibility, but that degree is always some distance from perfection. The Serial Stowaway is never not in danger of discovery. However, she is not afraid. The Serial Stowaway does not care about discovery, except as an inconvenience, or about the lack of discovery, except as a measure of the success of her invisibility efforts.

The movement that accompanies the initiation of this protective invisibility is a raising of her shoulders. When the need to be invisible is over, the shoulders lower.

So it was that when The Serial Stowaway became aware that the flight attendant had begun the task of checking passengers against her list of seat assignments, The Serial Stowaway's shoulders raised slightly. The flight attendant, her head rotating and bobbing from passengers to list with metronomic impersonality, approached. One row closer. Another row closer. When the flight attendant had gained a sightline to row twenty-one, she nodded from the row to her left to her list. She turned to her right. Her eyes swept across The Serial Stowaway. Her eyes landed on the passenger list. And the flight attendant paused. Her eyes went back to The Serial Stowaway and her seatmates, the ensconced man and the tweed-wearing man, and back to the list.

There are few forces as strong as the force that draws us toward a preordained outcome. Novelists and screenwriters know the power of this force, and place before their audiences at the outset of their stories hints of something dramatic that will happen in the future, assuming with good reason that we will follow the narrative with tongues hanging out until we reach this promised bit of drama.

To take a more everyday example, those who perform shift work know that the shift will end, and it is that knowledge, accompanied by a need for money resulting from the completion of that shift, that draws workers inexorably across the rough surface of their tasks in quest of the shift's thankfully inevitable end.

In this way, the flight attendant checking the passengers in their seats against a seating chart was in the grip of the inexorable force of the completion of that task. Anything that presented itself as a barrier to that completion had to meet a formidable threshold. Was the purported barrier real or illusory? Did it represent a minor or major error? Did it threaten the safety of the passengers? Did it threaten her employment? Did it require immediate action by her or reporting to someone else? Was a delay in answering these questions feasible, or even advisable, allowing her to do what she was so deeply drawn to do, which was to get to the end of this task?

These considerations hopping around in her mind, the flight attendant paused long enough for a clear view of a thin-faced woman, limp gray hair in a poorly executed mom-bob, her hands on her lap and gaze frontward as though contented to witness a mild-mannered minister deliver a not-particularly-compelling sermon, in row twenty-one, seat E, which according to the flight attendant's list was supposed to be empty.

Although certainly an anomaly, the situation did not have the power to resist the considerable force drawing the flight attendant to the conclusion of her task. What the situation warranted, the flight attendant delivered: a brief tightening of her lips, transitioning into a pursing of her lips, a light stroke of her writing implement on her paper, all within three seconds at the outside, followed by the continuation of her appointed rounds.

Because The Serial Stowaway kept her face toward the seatback in front of her, and because she willed her vision to go out of focus, she sensed rather than saw the flight attendant's pause, consideration, and continuation. Barely perceptibly, The Serial Stowaway's shoulders fell. Three seconds later, when The Serial Stowaway let her vision come back into focus and turned her head toward the aisle, she saw her seatmate's spiral notebook again disappearing into his inside jacket pocket and, peripherally, the flight attendant passing row twenty-one again in her return from aft to fore.

Two different flight attendants staffed the snack cart. At row twenty-one, to their right, the attendants tried halfheartedly, and failed, to get the attention of the ensconced man. The Serial Stowaway accepted a packet of cookies but declined a beverage. When the flight attendant held the packet of cookies toward the man in the aisle seat next to The Serial Stowaway, he shrugged and took it. When asked about a drink, he requested a cup of water. When both packet and cup were both placed on the man's lowered seat tray, he turned to The Serial Stowaway, a huge, proud smile lighting his face, and said, "You saw what I did there?"

He said these words loudly enough to be heard over the ambient aircraft noise; nonetheless, The Serial Stowaway, veteran listener to airplane conversations, leaned toward the man. The Serial Stowaway considered a moment, which was her wise habit, fools rushing in and all that, and said, "Well,

I saw you receive your cookies and drink."

"Correct," the man said, as if in triumph. "And did you happen to notice how I requested the receipt of these items?"

"I believe you said to the attendant, 'A cup of water, please.'"

"Right again," the man said. "And now," he said, and paused, index finger raised, as though he were a trial attorney preparing to deliver a crushing conclusion that would reveal to a rapt jury his manifestly guilty client's saintlike innocence, "did you happen to notice exactly how I requested the cookies?"

The Serial Stowaway took another moment for honest consideration and then, still leaning toward the man, said, "I believe you shrugged." She paused again. The man, mentally willing her to continue, waited. "You shrugged as if to say, 'Why not?' And the attendant handed you the packet."

"I believe, madam," the man declared, "that you are not just a seatmate but a colleague." He extended his arms in welcome, in doing so bumping his tray and nearly toppling his cup of water. "That is exactly what I did. I did not say, 'Yes, I would like that packet of cookies, please.' Rather, I used a gesture. But not the one you might expect. Not the more obvious nod of the head denoting the affirmative. No, I used a far more nuanced gesture, specifically, a shrug, which in this context and coupled with my smile, which you were not, I don't believe, in a position to see, communicated exactly the meaning you inferred: 'Why not?' And as a result, I received my cookies, which," he examined the packet, "look rather appetizing."

The Serial Stowaway nodded. Then she made a gesture of erasure with her right hand, made her face solemn, and replaced her nod with a shrug.

"Ah!" said the man in a tone at once delighted and pedantic. "By which you mean, 'I suppose so.' You are indeed a colleague." He removed his notebook and pen, turned to a page half-filled with handwriting, and added several words and what appeared to be a date. He did not return the notebook to his pocket, nor did he attend to his water or cookies. Rather, he leaned his head back and stared in whatever direction his eyes happened to point.

As he did so, The Serial Stowaway leaned forward and put her packet of cookies into the canvas bag under the seat in front of her. She would have enjoyed eating the cookies now, but she would appreciate them even more later.

When The Serial Stowaway resumed her upright position, the man began to speak, his posture suggesting he was speaking to himself. "I have been collecting evidence for quite some time," he said.

Given her avocation, we cannot blame The Serial Stowaway, hearing the phrase "collecting evidence," for experiencing an interest more than passing. The man seated next to her, had he been watching, would have been gratified to see that this surge manifested itself in a raising and lowering of the shoulders.

Almost spasmodically, the man turned his entire body toward The Serial Stowaway and said, "Perhaps you would appreciate hearing a sample of my findings."

The Serial Stowaway smiled and, with polite exaggeration, shrugged.

The man laughed. "Ah, yes. Why not? Why not, indeed." He lifted the notebook, still open to its most recent page, and drew the cover closed. He patted the cover once with affection and once with readiness, opened it again, and forefinger to paper, found a place to begin. Keeping his finger in place, he pinned The Serial Stowaway's eyes with his.

He raised his hand from the page, held the palm at eye level, then brought his hand down and took a beat. He made his face blank. Next, with care, he performed a shrug, on the heels of which he said, as though reciting a dictionary definition, "I don't know."

He raised his eyebrows as if asking whether The Serial Stowaway were following his method of presentation.

The Serial Stowaway nodded offhandedly.

Smiling, the man made a graceful gesture of releasing something into the wind, rather as a magician releases a white dove after having made it appear from a handkerchief.

An extended forefinger found a place in the notebook and then became part of a raised palm. Lowering the palm, the man again took a beat and made his face blank. He performed another shrug, this time amplified by a faint rolling of the shoulders, and recited another definition: "It doesn't matter."

He made the dove-releasing gesture, consulted his notebook, showed a palm, took his beat, and performed his shrug: "It doesn't matter much."

The releasing hand gesture this time was bumped out of

gracefulness by a passing young woman with a ponytail wearing a sweatshirt adorned with the giant red letters ASU behind which was a graphic representation of a sun. The man brought the hand down as though, bump or no bump, he had been meaning to do that, turned a page in his notebook, and drew his index finger along the entries. As before, he showed his palm, sought The Serial Stowaway's eyes, and erased his facial expression. He shrugged, then spoke the shrug's definition: "Oh well, mistakes happen."

The performance continued, interrupted once by the returning woman in the ASU sweatshirt, twice by the pair of flight attendants pushing the cart requesting trash, once by the pilot announcing the impending lighting of the seatbelt sign and need to return seat trays to their upright position preparatory to the still-thirty-minutes-away landing, and once by the slow passing of the flight attendant who had previously checked passengers against her list. At row twenty-one, she paused and seemed on the verge of speaking, but apparently not wanting to interrupt the deep communication obviously occurring between the man in the aisle seat and The Serial Stowaway, continued.

One shrug meant, "What else would you expect?"

Another shrug meant, "The same old thing."

Another: "Simply solved."

Another: "It's possible, but I doubt it."

Another: "What you say doesn't matter."

Another: "I guess that's the way it has to be."

Another: "I'm sorry."

Another: "I'm sorry to be the bearer of bad news."

Another: "If you insist, I will; it's not important."

Another: "If you insist, I will, but I'm not happy about it."

Another: "That isn't relevant."

Another: "I'd rather not say."

Another: "I don't know anything about that."

Another: "I know more about that than I am at liberty to say."

Another: "It doesn't matter if you believe me."

Another: "In a moment you're going to make me angry."

Another: "You're wrong, but I'm not going to bother to argue."

Another: "I'm not mad, but I am irritated."

Another: "It wasn't my fault."

Another: "I swear, I didn't do anything."

Another: "I'm not irritated anymore."

Another: "Simply solved; happy to help."

Another: "Simply solved; you could have figured it out by yourself."

Another: "I agree."

Another: "Only time will tell."

Another: "Whatever you say."

Another: "How was I to know?"

Another: "That's just the way things are."

Another: "I'll go along for now, but let's see how far this can go before it gets us in trouble."

Another: "I don't care."

Another: "I don't give a damn."

Another: "I care so much that I'm embarrassed."

Another: "You can have your way this time, but next time may be different."

Another: "Set that aside for now."

Another: "I don't know; that's the way I've always done it."

Another: "That's just the way it's done."

Another: "I'm no longer interested."

Another: "You can't take away my good humor."

Another: "I don't see any humor in that."

Another: "We're in no hurry."

Another: "Anyway, you're here."

Another: "It was worth a try."

Another: "Don't worry; he's cool."

Another shrug, this one more energetic: "All right, let it go."

Another shrug, this one a jerk up and down: "I don't want to think about it anymore."

Another shrug, this one threatening: "I don't want to talk about it anymore."

Another shrug, this one convulsive: "What could go wrong? Anything could go wrong."

Releasing the white dove one more time, the man turned forward, leaned back, and let his gaze float to top of the fuselage and perhaps, in his imagination, on to the clouds.

He maintained this posture when he resumed speaking, making his words audible to The Serial Stowaway only if she leaned her ear toward him, which she did only because when faced with a fifty/fifty decision, our lack of investment in either option does not relieve us from the need to select one.

The man said, "I am not terribly interested in shrugging as a merely functional movement. For example, were I to remove my sport jacket, you could say that I shrugged out of it. And if I put it back on, I would shrug into it. But these have no attraction for me. I am only slightly more interested in the origin of the shrug, but I confess I would not know how to conduct primary research on that point. Nonetheless, the existing literature is, if by necessity speculative, tantalizing, and to me anyway, it has the ring of truth."

The man closed his eyes. "The weight of scholarship leans toward the origin of shrugging as a primitive response to physical danger, such as a blow aimed toward the head." The man turned back toward The Serial Stowaway, and she, already leaning in his direction, turned toward him. A whirring and grinding sound announced the landing gear's emergence.

"The contemporary version of this sort of shrug," the man said, "for people fortunate enough to not be the subject of physical attack, is perhaps that gesture you see from people at a bus stop on the first cold day of winter—what we usually call a hunching of the shoulders."

His face clouded. "But we do sometimes see the more ancient form of shrugging, the warding off of a blow, actual or metaphorical. If you don't mind my saying so, I witnessed an example of this sort of shrug from you earlier in our flight. As the flight attendant approached holding what I assumed to be the passenger list, your shoulders raised. Not abruptly, not drastically, but with what I took to be an instinctive quality. Further, your shoulders remained raised, which is not characteristic of the modern shrug, but is characteristic of a shrug the peak of which is maintained until the expected blow falls, or until the blow does not fall, in which case the shoulders descend, as yours did when the flight attendant and her list passed."

The man sighed. "I am not inclined to explain why people shrug, nor to posit relationships among the different applications of shrugging. I leave that to those whose minds cannot be at peace with observations but require the false comfort of conclusions. Camille Debras of the University Paris Nanterre, for example, in her article 'The shrug: Forms and meanings of a compound enactment' in the journal *Gesture*, defined shrugging as a network of forms unified by a common semantic theme of personal disengagement. For my part, I have only one simple interpretation to offer: If the origin of the shrug as a defensive gesture is correct, then the rather obvious conclusion is that a gesture that began as an impotent reaction to danger has evolved into one that largely expresses degrees of apathy. I am certain that my rather simple conclusion—really, it is barely more than an observation—could be elaborated on by Dr. Debras and others with more energy and intelligence than I—those with a sense of duty toward conclusions. Any duty I feel is limited to the far more modest activity of making the little notes in my notebook, where, I hope you don't mind, I recorded your most interesting shrug."

Although this man's sense of duty was an episodic sort, other types of duty pull one as inexorably toward a conclusion as readers are drawn to witness Tom Sawyer and Becky Thatcher emerge safely from the cave.

For the flight attendant in charge of comparing the passengers seated in the airplane with the passengers printed on the list, once she had obeyed the lure to complete her task uninterrupted, the lure of duty took over. And duty, as she finally construed it by the time the wheels of the plane touched the runway, required that, when the plane was at the gate but before the doors had opened, she tell the pilot about the discrepancy she had noted: an unaccounted-for passenger in row twenty-one, seat E.

Therefore, when the passengers, after some delay, deplaned, each with that blinking of momentary confusion at emerging into a scene so different from that so recently occupied, the flight attendant with the passenger list was stationed at the gate. And when The Serial Stowaway emerged, her limp canvas bag on her shoulder and the man in the notebook-containing tweed sport coat behind her, the attendant nodded at her, and a somber-faced man and woman, both in starched white shirts and black polyester pants with center pleats looking sharp enough to slit skin, appeared from seemingly nowhere. The woman took The Serial Stowaway's elbow and led her two steps to the right, where they paused, the officers facing The Serial Stowaway.

The man in the tweed sport coat, witnessing this maneuver, slowed his pace and adjusted his direction so as to have a side view of the action.

Later, he would wonder whether The Serial Stowaway had looked at him from the corner of her eye, or whether that was just his fancy—a bad habit for one whose avocation is objective observation. The man in the sport coat was sure, however, of one thing he saw.

Facing her inquisitors, soon to be her accusers, The Serial Stowaway shrugged.

The man continued through the gate area. At a water fountain, he stopped and reached for his notebook. Before he touched the notebook, however, he let his arm fall to his side in a gesture of helplessness one might say was analogous to a shrug.

Chapter 2:
The Serial Stowaway
and the Abstract Executive

On a mid-May morning, its brightness apparent through the ample windows at Chicago's O'Hare Airport, in the line toward security checkpoint fifteen, The Serial Stowaway maneuvered to stand beside a silver-haired man wearing aviator sunglasses, a Panama hat, and a Caesar's Palace bathrobe tied loosely over his clothes. At the acrylic-covered TSA kiosk, as the agent asked the man to remove his sunglasses, and as passengers at adjacent checkpoints engaged the man in banter about his bathrobe, The Serial Stowaway glided past and into a line toward a baggage-scanning belt, where, as she waited for her nearly empty canvas tote to emerge from the screening device, she watched one of the agents lift from a suitcase a plastic witch's head stuck on a plastic drill.

At the gate area for a flight to Atlanta, The Serial Stowaway slipped past the boarding-pass checkpoint while the attendant was explaining to a young man that the pillowcase he

was holding in addition to his duffle bag constituted an unauthorized second carry-on item because the pillowcase contained not a pillow but clothing, toiletries, and a microphone.
As she entered the gangway, The Serial Stowaway heard the
man argue at high volume that he planned to rest his head on
the contents of the pillowcase, and because it would function
as a pillow it was no different than a pillow, technically.

Emerging from a bathroom several minutes after an announcement asking everyone to find and take their seats in
preparation for takeoff, The Serial Stowaway at first was concerned she had boarded a completely full flight until she saw
an empty middle seat three rows behind the curtains that rendered first-class passengers unseen from the great unwashed
and vice versa. Momentarily dislodging a man in an electric
blue suit but no necktie on his white shirt, she slid into place
and deposited her tote under the seatback in front of her, as
the blue-suited man resumed his place in the aisle seat, wrig-
gled to get comfortable, and crossed his legs, placing his right
calf, ankle, and shoe directly in the path of a band of sunlight,
as though a spotlight had flickered on, suggesting to the audience that this portion of the man's body was poised to do
something remarkable. Seeming to acquiesce, the foot began
to wiggle—from left to right, not too quickly, not too slowly.

Her many airplane trips had made The Serial Stowaway a
regular observer of the lower calves, ankles, and shoes of her
seatmates, those being more natural things on which her eyes
to rest than faces, which require a forty-five degree head turn
and which, far more often than a smile, return expressions of
puzzlement, annoyance, or guilt, drawing more attention to

The Serial Stowaway than she deemed wise.

The calf-ankle-shoe design spotlighted by this morning's May sun was not unknown to The Serial Stowaway, but never had been quite so perfectly spotlighted. Although not a sports fan, The Serial Stowaway nonetheless saw in the calf-ankle-shoe a resemblance to a hockey stick—rigid, thin, and pointed sharply up and to the right. Had The Serial Stowaway shared this impression with the electric-blue-suited man, we might infer that he would have smiled with gratitude, a hockey stick shape being very desirable when depicted in line graphs depicting highly positive sales performance, a type of graph that a person of this man's attire is likely to view monthly if not more frequently. Witnessing a graph with such a shape, the wiggling of his foot would have been correctly interpreted as a sign of excitement.

The man would have been less pleased by the next phase in The Serial Stowaway's assessment. As a shape, the calf-ankle-shoe may have resembled a hockey stick, but as a calf, ankle, and shoe they resembled those of a clown—the tightness of the pant leg accentuating both the thinness of the calf and the comic elongation of the shoe. The electric blue of the pant leg was suitably bright for a clown's garb, and the incongruity of the buttery soft tan leather of the shoe's upper with its white gym-shoe sole may not have been slapstick but was farcical.

Had the man's ankle been covered by a brightly colored, horizontally striped sock, the clown comparison would have been even more apt, but the lower leg and ankle that protruded from the pant leg were covered by nothing except long, fine, sparse, ginger-colored hairs sprouted from pale skin and sparkling as they caught the sunlight.

As the man's foot wiggle shifted from left to right to up and down, changing the way in which the sunlight sparkled on his leg hair, The Serial Stowaway's peripheral vision caught another motion: a flight attendant making her way down the aisle checking the occupied seats against her passenger list. The Serial Stowaway had been ready to look at something besides this man's calf-ankle-shoe, but thought it wise to keep her gaze there so as to not invite the flight attendant to meet The Serial Stowaway's eyes. The gambit seemed to work, or perhaps the flight attendant was busy or didn't care or, more likely, had the same disinclination to pause and examine something incongruous as children practicing a musical instrument as a parent-ordered prerequisite to going outside to play. Which did not mean The Serial Stowaway would not be identified, stopped, reproved, threatened, remanded, just that it would not happen at this moment.

When the plane began to taxi, the beam of light departed, and the man uncrossed his legs.

Hearing the plane's engine begin a crescendo, The Serial Stowaway faced forward and prepared for the sensation of takeoff, which to her, on this flight, resembled a slow wipe transition in a film, only instead of one image being replaced with another, one image, the back of the seat in front of her, was replaced by a field of gray, unpopulated as of yet by anything except gray, a gray that, to The Serial Stowaway, would be sufficient if no other image appeared.

As the captain announced the flight had reached cruising altitude, The Serial Stowaway heard a sigh from her right—whether of preparation or resignation she did not know—and turned to see the electric-blue-suited man lean forward and reach under the seat in front of him. He emerged holding a slender bag that matched the leather of his shoes, from which he withdrew a laptop computer. Once the man had replaced the bag, The Serial Stowaway saw that her comparison of him to a hockey stick was valid only from the knees down.

Above that point, particularly in the contours of belly and face, the blue-suited man showed incipient chubbiness that no doubt had been hinted in the man's thirties and was establishing its position now in the man's early forties, preparing for slow advancement in the coming decades, perhaps to be intermittently beaten back by diet and exercise.

Laptop in one hand, the blue-suited man lowered the tray table, placed the laptop on it, and paused with what to The Serial Stowaway seemed either the reverence of one about to open a prayer book, or the trepidation of one about to open a letter one suspects contains bad news. Then his fingers tapped what seemed a glissando, and The Serial Stowaway could see, even from her angle, bright rectangles containing images, shapes, and words appear on the screen.

Next, the man made a gesture with three fingers extended, and the clutter on the screen disappeared. He made one click, and a large, white rectangle appeared, having, as best The Serial Stowaway could see, small blocks of text widely spaced from top to bottom of the white space.

The man appeared to study the screen for several seconds, then closed his eyes. The man's lips began to move, but if any sound emerged, it was too quiet for The Serial Stowaway to hear over the ambient noise of the airplane.

Eventually, The Serial Stowaway turned to her left, rewarded by a view of a woman wearing a baseball cap with a bill as elongated as the blue-suited man's foot. Then, The Serial Stowaway let her eyes travel to wherever they chose to visit.

At the flight attendant's beverage inquiry, the blue-suited man started as if realizing he was doing in public something usually private, recovered, and asked for a Coke and, smiling sheepishly, an extra packet of pretzels. The Serial Stowaway took pretzels, declined a beverage, placed her pretzels in the seatback for when her hunger was more demanding, and sat back, marginally aware of the man alternating his munching and sipping, with screen-studying and eye-closing.

Her gaze returned to her seatback, The Serial Stowaway became aware that the munching and sipping had stopped, and that the screen-studying, eye-closing, and lip-moving were now interspersed with glances her way, at first brief and surreptitious, then more direct and inviting.

Finally, the blue-suited man paused in his look at The Serial Stowaway to obviously invite her participation, and when The Serial Stowaway met the invitation halfway, the man said, the sheepish expression he had given the flight attendant having evolved into something both more pleasant and imploring, "Say."

The Serial Stowaway's silence was apparently to the man

the equivalent of her saying "Yes?" for he continued. "Say, I wonder. I wonder if you might be willing to help me with something. I mean, it's not something, really, it's nothing. I wonder," he spoke quickly now, "would you be willing to help me rehearse?"

The Serial Stowaway wondered whether he was an actor. His voice certainly was smooth enough for an actor's voice—with a sort of subtle rounding not unlike the blue-suited man's cheeks.

The man continued, "I'm on my way to a job interview. A big interview. For a big job. I'm asking if you would help me rehearse for the interview. I shouldn't have said 're-hearse.' I should have said 'practice.' He ducked his head in a gesture of self-deprecation equal parts practiced and genu-ine. "Sometimes I use the wrong words."

The Serial Stowaway nodded gravely and opened a palm as if to say, "Do go on."

The man gestured back toward the screen. "The ques-tions are here. Anyway, the questions I suspect they'll ask. Or I hope they'll ask. Mostly everyone asks the same questions."

The Serial Stowaway had not had a job interview in forty-one years but was only mildly curious how they were conducted these days.

The man lifted the laptop and held it toward The Serial Stowaway, who lowered her tray table to receive the device.

"I've been rehearsing by myself," the man continued, as The Serial Stowaway assessed the words on the screen before her. "But I think it would help to say my responses out loud, to another person. You know, things always sound good in your head, but sometimes not so good when you say them."

The man interrupted himself to say, "I'm sorry. I wouldn't ask if I thought you were busy with something. But you didn't seem to be doing anything in particular."

The Serial Stowaway hadn't been doing anything she could easily explain, or anything that would be evident to others, but she had been doing something. She had been experiencing an airplane ride. She had been experiencing the sensation of traveling from one place to another. She had been experiencing the sensation between going away and going toward—the delicate balance of those sensations and its continuous and almost imperceptible shift as the flight progressed.

She shrugged, said, "Surely," and looked more closely at the words on the screen, which, she now saw, were questions separated by wide bands of blank space.

"Just," the man gestured, "read the first one."

The Serial Stowaway squinted and read. "Good afternoon, Richard. Would you tell me a bit about yourself?"

To which the man, staring at the seat back before him, said, "Please, call me Rich. Yes, I'd be happy to. I'm a senior business development and marketing executive who creates long-term value through innovative strategies that drive reputation, relationships, and revenue." He turned to The Serial Stowaway and nodded toward the screen.

Consulting the next block of text, The Serial Stowaway said, "Could you," she paused, cocking her head, "flush that out for me?" Images of a toilet and a skeleton in her mind, she wondered if that word should have been "flesh" rather than "flush," but knew that, once she started to change the questions, she would be accepting a level of responsibility greater than her desired level of investment.

The man called Rich replied, "Certainly. I'm a seasoned executive with more than twenty-five years of industry and global professional services experience transforming businesses through innovative go-to-market strategies, large-scale program management, strategic relationship-building, and brand elevation. My areas of expertise include business development, sales enablement, stakeholder management, business strategy and planning, change management, HR and talent management, operational excellence, program management, knowledge management, solution development, thought leadership, and learning and development." He nodded again toward the screen.

The Serial Stowaway located her place and read, "Could you tell me how you go about transforming businesses?"

"Yes, indeed. First, I catalyze explosive business growth. I have a proven track record of boosting market penetration and maximizing revenue, including contributing to the growth of a global professional services business from about one point five billion to four point four billion dollars in revenue."

The man named Rich began to cross his legs, but his knee bumped the tray table, tipping over his cup and spilling the drops of remaining from his Coke-tinged melted ice. Shaking his head in a facsimile of tolerable embarrassment, he wiped up the drops, stashed the cup, napkin, and pretzel wrapper in the seat-back pouch, and raised the tray. He completed his leg-crossing before continuing, his foot wiggling slowly left to right. "Also, I drive sales success from planning to execution, consistently leading to business wins through the cultivation of trusted partnerships and exceptional stakeholder management at the C-suite level and beyond. I deeply listen to and understand root issues and collaborate to deliver customized solutions. I seamlessly manage large, complex programs and optimize operational efficiency to enhance brands and grow revenue across geographies, accounts, programs, and solutions. To that end, I embrace technology and digital channels to enact positive go-to-market strategies, programs, and solutions that maximize return on investment."

The foot wiggle paused, then resumed, now faster, now up and down.

"Also, I adeptly lead and expand global, cross-functional teams through periods of significant disruption. To do that, I foster collaborative cultures, and I passionately engage in coaching and developing the next generation of diverse leaders. I should add that I'm a life sciences and health industry expert and thought leader who is proficient in the entire life sciences value chain. I have a reputation for identifying emerging industry trends and successfully navigating regulatory challenges within the highly complex and dynamic sector landscape. I develop and promote market-leading industry brands and insights and am a sought-after speaker and author."

The man named Rich looked toward The Serial Stowaway, his smile, a bit lopsided this time, seeming to gauge her interest.

The Serial Stowaway had not been able to hear every word of this response over the normal airplane noise. What she had heard had sounded lovely. She pictured words, most recognizable, being tossed high into the air and falling gently, forming and reforming into random groups that stripped away the meaning of the words and left something abstract and animated, as if sparkling stars were drifting down from a night sky.

The Serial Stowaway nodded. "Well, that's wonderful."

The man named Rich smiled shyly, then nodded toward the laptop screen.

The Serial Stowaway read, "Please tell us about your duties and accomplishments in your current position."

After a pause to hand his cup, wrapper, and napkin to the passing flight attendant, who transferred them into her garbage bag, the man named Rich paused, seeming to gather his thoughts, and spoke: "For the past nineteen years I've been with a professional services firm operating in one hundred and forty countries with over four hundred thousand professionals. I've directly contributed to the growth and transformation of this firm into a fifty-billion-dollar organization recognized on Fortune's 100 Best Companies to Work list for twenty-five years in a row. For the past five years my title has been Global Health Sciences and Wellness Knowledge Leader reporting to the Global HS and W Leader. I am responsible for the knowledge function across the entirety of the four-point-four-billion-dollar HS and W global practice, utilizing expertise in operational planning and execution and people and program management. In this role, I manage a global team of nearly eighty professionals to support all HS and W initiatives."

He turned to The Serial Stowaway, who had been distracted by the appearance of not just words but now letters falling from the sky and forming their own pleasing groups. Placing her attention back on the screen and locating her place, she realized she had come to the last question. She pointed toward the screen. The man named Rich uncrossed his legs, looked at the screen, then reached over and touched something that made the words crawl up.

"You're really very kind to do this," he said.

The Serial Stowaway resumed reading. "Could you tell us what you have accomplished in this role?"

"I can," Rich replied, recrossing his legs and beginning to wiggle his foot, up and down this time, and faster than before. "I refer to these," Rich said, "as transformational accomplishments. I transformed the knowledge function to help accelerate the firm's brand, market penetration, and revenue growth. Specifically, I built and managed teams of analysts to provide vital research, analysis, thought leadership, and industry learning, customizing hiring and training based on unique sub-sector, functional, and technical needs. In addition, I nurtured strong partnerships with HS and W leaders to advance their strategic goals, maximizing market impact by understanding needs and aligning the right resources to effectively influence and deliver value to their clients. Also, I utilized my strong executive presence to drive sales and support global projects; driving million-dollar opportunities as an account sales executive and tapping into C-suite executives to drive the firm's external POVs." His foot stopped wiggling, and the man named Rich said, "Oh." He turned to The Serial Stowaway. Again, he said, "Oh," this time elaborating: "I suppose you don't know what a POV is."

The Serial Stowaway, who had been lulled by the man's voice fading in and out of the ambient airplane noise, adding to the sense of abstraction in the words and letters, had heard the letters "POV" but had enjoyed not feeling any need to know their meaning.

"Points of view," the man said and for no obvious reason smiled sadly. "Statements of ideas about various issues."

The first-class curtain parted, and through the opening appeared the flight attendant who had originally checked passengers against the passenger list. A piece of paper in her hand, she stood a moment, surveying the first few rows, perhaps paying special attention to the row containing the man in the electric blue suit and The Serial Stowaway. She began to walk down the aisle.

The Serial Stowaway, making her voice sound official, said, "Thank you, Rich. Do continue."

Rich smiled, indicating he was in on the joke, but it was a weak smile. He took a breath, wiggled his foot faster than ever, and continued. "Also, I embedded customized analysis into projects across the entire client sales cycle, achieving differential insights resulting in substantially more C-suite meetings, increased RFPs..." he paused, looked at The Serial

Stowaway from the corner of his eyes, said, "requests for pro-posals," and continued, "mm, let's see, bigger wins and fol-low-on sales for our firm's account teams. In addition, I co-created and program-managed global priority solutions and business development campaigns—novel, digital projects that successfully opened doors to new and existing custom-ers."

He gestured again toward the screen. The Serial Stowa-way consulted the words, found her place, and said, "Would you like to tell us about any other accomplishments?"

"Yes. I fostered a culture of peer knowledge sharing, in-creasing visibility and communication among cross-func-tional teams, maximizing firm intelligence and speed-to-mar-ket. In addition, I embedded new technologies, including AI…" He paused, said to The Serial Stowaway, "artificial in-telligence—I may not stop to define each of these. I wish I could. I hope I'm not being rude. The interviewer will know what all these things mean. Um, AI methods, and resources into projects, providing quicker access to internal and exter-nal information resulting in increased operational efficiencies and sales opportunities. And finally, I provided global HS and W leaders with distinct industry-leading insights, trends, and thought leadership, in client interactions, industry con-ferences, within marquee reports, and for media and PR pro-motion. At this point, I am myself considered a prominent smee within the company."

The Serial Stowaway, who had enjoyed individual words and letters forming new and unfamiliar groupings, was de-lighted to now hear what seemed to be a sound that she had never previously heard. She said, "Smee?

Rich turned to The Serial Stowaway. "S.M.E. Subject-matter expert."

His foot no longer wiggled. He gestured toward the screen. The Serial Stowaway shook her head, and Rich reached out and advanced the document.

The Serial Stowaway found her place and resumed her reading. "I see that early in your career you were a pharmacy sales representative."

"Yes, as a hospital sales representative and district trainer for an American privately held pharmacy company, I influenced the prescribing habits of targeted health professionals, including internists, oncologists, surgeons, and anesthesiologists at accounts including the teaching hospitals of Harvard Medical School."

The Serial Stowaway said, "It looks like that's all."

The Serial Stowaway handed back the laptop and raised her seat tray. The man stored the device. As the two settled back, The Serial Stowaway tried to create a picture of what the man named Rich and his colleagues did at work, visualizing many rooms full of people typing on their laptops, words and letters drifting from the ceiling, coalescing and separating and coalescing again.

The flight attendant with the paper passed again as the seatbelt sign lighted, accompanied by the usual electronic bell tone.

As if that were a cue, the man called Rich said, "I didn't include that question about why I'm looking for a new position."

Seeing that Rich was not looking at her, The Serial Stowaway did not bother to nod.

The pilot made his announcement about the flight attendants making one last round through the cabin in preparation for landing.

The flight attendant who had previously collected trash came by with another floppy plastic bag. The attendant with the paper stood at the threshold to first class, as if blocking it.

The Serial Stowaway closed her eyes. As she had when the plane was about to take off, she let the wipe transition take place, replacing the words and letters that the man named Rich had caused to float from the sky with the field of gray.

"It's not anything you can actually see." The man named Rich was speaking. "You can't point to any one thing. Not to something a person says or to a look someone gives you or to someone getting a promotion that should have been yours, or anything like that."

The Serial Stowaway kept her eyes forward but leaned toward the man named Rich. He was not speaking loudly. He may have been speaking to himself.

"It's more what is not said. The quality of the silence. An emptiness in the air. It's terrible. It's frightening. You know. People stop looking at you. Talk stops when you walk into a room. You know that the floor you're standing on will be taken away. The walls around you. The roof. And you will be alone, completely alone. Not alone like walking on a beach alone. Alone like a toddler alone in an empty lot."

He turned toward The Serial Stowaway. "The last couple of times, I moved to a different department. But this time there is nowhere left in that company for me to be safe. So now it's a matter of getting away as quickly as I can, getting away before whatever is going to happen happens. Or maybe nothing will happen. But I'm too frightened to wait. Except even with this interview, all I can do is wait to see if I get the job." He crossed his legs as he had when he first sat, highlighting calf, bare ankles, and elongated shoe. "And," he said, "my ankles are cold."

The Serial Stowaway heard the man's words, but they did not register. The Serial Stowaway had thoughts of her own. Soon they would be on the ground, taxiing toward the gate. That was when the pilot welcomed the passengers to the destination city. This was also when the pilot sometimes made an additional announcement. That announcement, when made, went something like this: "When we reach the gate, everyone please remain seated. There's a matter we need to attend to on board before anyone can deplane." And sometimes the pilot did not say anything. All The Serial Stowaway could do was wait.

Chapter 3:
The Serial Stowaway
and the Texas Ranger

In the small conference room that doubled as an interrogation room, before sitting where indicated by one of three Dallas Love Field airport security officers, the one with the gold-colored five-pointed star pinned to his starched white shirt, The Serial Stowaway gave the chair an appraising look.

Only a few minutes before, The Serial Stowaway had been delivered to this room and this star-wearing man by two other security officers. The star-wearing man had a face clean-shaven even at two p.m., and seemed to The Serial Stowaway to be young, short, and slight for one of his rank. The two other officers, who stood nearby in a reasonable approximation of being at the ready, were taller, older, and stockier than the supervisor. One was a man whose lips were tightly pursed, the other a woman whose lips appeared ready for either a sneer or a smile, the dark skin of both a stark contrast to the white of their shirts, the white of the walls, and the white of the supervisor's shiny skin. Neither of these two officers wore a star.

In a voice that a reasonable person would judge to have been modeled after a television football coach or rancher, those models, however, being unattainable by a voice so thin, the supervisor had instructed the female officer to search the person of The Serial Stowaway and the male officer to search her bag, and for the results to be placed on the glass-top conference table. The former search yielded two airline napkins and three dollar bills. The latter found within The Serial Stowaway's limp canvas tote two packets of airline cookies and a paper menu from the Hearth Locavore Kitchen on Concourse A North of the Kansas City International Airport with a handful of curved lines in various colors of crayon drawn in a space between the Breakfast Sammy and the Avocado Toast.

Eyeing this meager evidence with mildly concealed disgust, the supervisor waved his older, taller, stockier, darker subordinates to stand against the wall and waved The Serial Stowaway into a conference-room chair, the one she gave an appraising look.

At this point in The Serial Stowaway's career, she had spent enough hours in enough such rooms tucked into enough hallways in enough airports, and in these rooms, she had sat in enough conference room chairs, that she had formed a theory governing her impression of these chairs. That theory was as follows: All comfortable conference room chairs were alike, but all uncomfortable conference room chairs were uncomfortable in their own way.

The Serial Stowaway had worked out this concept in a bit

more detail while passing the night in the Oklahoma City Airport.

The elements of discomfort in a conference room chair coalesced into five categories. One was softness: Some of the chairs had seats hard, unyielding, and flat enough to cause real pain, particularly for one such as The Serial Stowaway who lacked posterior padding. Another category was height: Some chairs were so low that the conference table she faced was chest height, and some were so high her feet didn't touch the ground unless she extended her toes. Another category was pitch: Some chairs reclined so far back that she had to lean forward to touch the table, and some pitched so far forward she felt at risk for falling onto the table. Another category was adjustability: Some chairs had controls for modifying back angle, tilt degree, tilt tension, tilt lock, lumbar support, arm height, and seat height, thereby promising the ultimate in tailored sitting experience. The last category was workability: In many chairs having adjustment capability, the controls had the propensity to fling the seated person up, down, forward, or back in a way that was at least undignified and at most dangerous, while others had controls that were so difficult to either find or operate that the seated person might be brought to tears before either figuring out how to adjust the chair or begging for an operator's manual to consult.

The more comfortable chairs were generally favorable in all of these characteristics. The uncomfortable chairs, on the other hand, tended to be most prominently unfavorable in one of the five categories. It was almost as though the people who selected these chairs in the various airport security departments in the various cities across the country had orchestrated their chair selections so that those sitting in each chair in each room were poked with different sticks of different weights from different directions.

Just after the security supervisor motioned The Serial Stowaway into this conference room chair, just after The Serial Stowaway glanced appraisingly at this chair, and just before she sat, The Serial Stowaway for no particular reason glanced back toward the supervisor. When she did so, her eyes landed on the gold star pinned to his shirt. At that moment it occurred to The Serial Stowaway that this star was the perfect graphic representation of her system of conference-room-chair evaluation. Each point on the five-pointed star proudly declared a specific point of discomfort with which a specific chair would torment its captive.

Take this chair, for example, the one offered by the officer wearing the star, the one into which The Serial Stowaway now attempted to settle. This chair was so low that The Serial Stowaway felt like a child at a grown-up table. She imagined seeing one point of the gold star on the security officer's shirt throb with pride.

Not displaying any problem with the chair height despite his own limited stature, the supervisor sat and introduced himself as Airport Security Sergeant Clinton Peoples. Fingering his star badge, he said, "I was named after a famous Texas Ranger." He dropped his hand from the badge and glanced with fleeting embarrassment toward the two officers standing along the wall. Attention back to The Serial Stowaway, he said, "You can call me Clint."

The Serial Stowaway said, "Hello, Clint."

Sergeant Peoples nodded gravely. "And what can I call you, ma'am?"

The Serial Stowaway said, "You may call me, hmm, Marjorie, Clint."

Sergeant Peoples nodded soberly. "And what would be your last name, Marjorie?"

The Serial Stowaway gave a surname beginning with the letter M that she forgot after saying it.

Sergeant Peoples nodded pensively. Then he glanced to the officers standing by the wall as if to ensure they, too, were pensive.

Returning to The Serial Stowaway, he offered something to drink, and she requested water. When the female officer had been dispensed to fulfill this request and had returned, and The Serial Stowaway had taken two sips, the questioning resumed.

Sergeant Peoples, at every transition of topic tweaking his gold star and glancing toward his standing subordinates while The Serial Stowaway shifted the leg beneath her in the low chair, embarked on questions familiar to The Serial Stowaway:

Where do you live, Marjorie?

Where did you grow up, Marjorie?

Where does your family live, Marjorie? (Why, The Serial Stowaway always wondered, this obsession with place?)

Do you have a husband or children, Marjorie?

Do you have a job, Marjorie?

What are your plans in Dallas, Marjorie?

The Serial Stowaway appreciated Sergeant Peoples' liberal use of her name. It made her feel liked and valued; it also helped her remember which name she had chosen. She used the name Clint frequently in her answers for no reason other than it seemed the polite thing to do.

With the same care he would use if stalking a deer in the woods, Sergeant Peoples approached the day's events.

Where is your identification, Marjorie?

Where is your boarding pass, Marjorie?

How did you get past TSA in Chicago, Marjorie?

How did you board the plane, Marjorie?

With a tweak of his star and a glance at his observing officers, he broadened his questions.

Marjorie, is this the first time you have boarded a plane without a ticket?

Marjorie, how many times have you done it?

And, of course, the inevitable finale: Marjorie, why do you do it?

The Serial Stowaway always was surprised at the lack of insistence from her interrogators on answers concrete or cogent, or even answers at all. To Sergeant Peoples' questions, The Serial Stowaway alternated among tested responses.

A smile accompanied by a wave of her hand.

"Oh, Clint, that's a long story."

"Well, Clint, that's complicated."

"Now Clint, I'm sure you don't have the time for all that."

Eventually, after a restroom break for The Serial Stowaway and a much longer break for Sergeant Peoples, he returned to the conference room and gave orders. The male officer, lips still pursed, was assigned to photograph and fingerprint The Serial Stowaway. That done, Sergeant Peoples handed a slip of paper to the female officer, her lips rigidly fixed between smile and sneer, and instructed her to escort The Serial Stowaway back to the airport concourse and thence onto this flight back—he pointed at the slip of paper—to Chicago. Sergeant Peoples, for the first time in their exchange using a tone that approached scolding, informed The Serial Stowaway that she would be expected to reimburse the airline for the return flight.

The female officer guided The Serial Stowaway outside the door of the security office, into the hidden hallway, and onto the concourse, where she stopped and consulted the piece of paper. As a smattering of people walked around them, the female officer told The Serial Stowaway that they had plenty of time to eat before the flight and that the only tolerable choice among the sorry options for eating at Love Field was Bruegger's Bagels. "The best thing about Bruegger's Bagels," the officer said, "is that it's near the front door, so we can step outside for fresh air." The officer also told The Serial Stowaway the worst thing about Bruegger's Bagels, but that piece of information was drowned out by a public-address announcement threatening anyone intending to take a certain flight to Atlanta with abandonment if they did not immediately board a plane whose doors were poised to close.

The officer kept slightly behind and to one side of The Serial Stowaway, guiding her with the words "there" and "here," but not by touch. The corridor toward Bruegger's Bagels and fresh air was wide but low-ceilinged. However, when they passed beneath a mezzanine, the ceiling lifted dramatically. The Serial Stowaway stopped. Despite the increase in ceiling height, it was only barely tall enough to accommodate the figure The Serial Stowaway faced.

The officer pulled up to her side.

The thing appeared to be the back of a huge, bronze man on a brown marble pedestal. The Serial Stowaway still did not move.

"The bagels are around this thing," the officer said. Recognizing her cue, The Serial Stowaway began the process of circumnavigation.

As they rounded the statue, The Serial Stowaway saw a TSA security station, a Cinnabon, and, yes, there, the long black rectangle on which blocky, serif, white letters announced the presence of Bruegger's Bagels.

Yet neither the allure of bagels—and The Serial Stowaway was hungry—nor the possibility of applying her five-point chair-discomfort tool to assessing the seats at the Bruegger's Bagels could overcome the gravitational pull of the thing in the center of the lobby.

When they had fully rounded the massive thing and were facing their destination, The Serial Stowaway had no choice. She stopped. She turned. And she looked up to the very top of the thing.

She saw the towering bronze sweep of a giant Stetson hat.

Beneath that emerged neatly clipped bronze hair, a milky face, and eyes unnervingly bland.

Beneath that were graceful folds of shirt draped from broad, bronze shoulders,

On the shirt, above the shirt's button-flap chest pocket, was a five-pointed star within a narrow circle, a bronze version of the gold star pinned in the same position on the white shirt of security supervisor Sergeant Peoples.

The thing's left arm and hand hung loosely over the handle of a holstered pistol, surely imposing enough in real life but in this reproduction looking like a combination club and gun.

The thing's right arm was outstretched, palm down, ready to either pat or concuss the head of a person unreasonable enough to express any signs of discontent with the current state.

Bronze uniform pants, somehow both tight and draped, defined muscular legs, one standing erect but relaxed, boot planted on a puddle of bronze, the other with knee extended and boot heel raised, as if in the middle of an insouciant stride.

Below the boots, not far below The Serial Stowaway's eye level, was a feces-brown marble pedestal. On the pedestal was engraved another five-pointed star. This was not the five-pointed star of Officer Peoples' badge. It was not the five-pointed star representing the pokes and prods of uncomfortable chairs sat in during interrogations fatuous and inconvenient. It was not threatening in a vague way. This star, crude and huge, as though engraved in anger by someone with the tools to translate that anger into action, was explicit in its threat.

Between the points were awkwardly rendered letters spelling TEXAS.

The Serial Stowaway's gaze was drawn past the five-pointed star in the same way that an audience knows it will only be free from a tragic opera by allowing it to carry on to its horrible conclusion, that conclusion in this case being these words engraved at the base of the pedestal:

TEXAS RANGER OF 1960
"ONE RIOT, ONE RANGER"

To The Serial Stowaway's right came the officer's voice. "Bluster," the voice said. Turning toward the officer, The Serial Stowaway wondered why she had not previously noticed the gorgeously asymmetrical pile of braids on the officer's head. "Hubris," the officer continued, not expressing any emotion, just stating facts. "Hauteur." The officer gestured behind her and said, "Bagels."

They swiveled to face Bruegger's Bagels, The Serial Stowaway trying to decide whether this Bruegger's Bagels looked comically small compared with the bronze thing or whether the bronze thing looked comically large compared with the Bruegger's Bagels, or whether the disparity was not particularly comical from either vantage point.

The officer addressed the young woman at the counter as Isabel, or perhaps Isabella, and the young woman at the counter addressed the officer as Charline, confirmed she wanted the usual, and put in an order for lox and cream cheese on onion-pumpernickel bagel, not toasted, while the officer selected a gigantic can of Arizona Iced Tea from a nearby cooler. The officer gestured for The Serial Stowaway to order, but The Serial Stowaway had some difficulty persuading the young woman at the counter that she wanted nothing but turkey on her bagel and that she wanted no type of bagel other than plain and that she wanted nothing to drink besides the smallest available bottle of water, which could not really be described as small in any context other than that of drink sizes at airports.

The security officer guided The Serial Stowaway into the lobby, which contained no seats, and through electric-eye-operated glass doors to a blast of moist heat and the sound of car and plane engines that seemed to manifest themselves tactilely as grit in the air. They ate sitting on a concrete bench with huge standing ashtrays on either side. The Serial Stowaway ate half of her sandwich and deposited the other half in her canvas tote. The officer, having finished her sandwich, deposited the wrapper in a concrete-encased can next to the nearest ashtray, returned to the bench, leaned back as though the bench were a reclining chair, closed her eyes, and sipped from her can of Arizona Iced Tea.

Without opening her eyes, the officer said, "My name is Officer Charline Jordan. Sergeant Peoples did not see the need to introduce me previously."

The Serial Stowaway said, "My name is not," she paused to recall the name she had given, "Marjorie."

"I get that," Officer Jordan said. Eventually, she turned

to The Serial Stowaway, who saw that the officer's lips were completely at rest in their state between sneer and smile. "I suppose," she said, "I am going to have to explain that statue to yet another Yankee." She sighed as if bored, or, perhaps more precisely, as if she wished she were bored. She started at the statue's base.

The words, she explained, were the motto of The Texas Rangers. There was, no matter what the motto said, no riot. It was a boxing match. The mayor of a town called Langtry called for the Texas Rangers to come in and break up an illegal boxing match. The mayor, Officer Jordan said, met the train, from which emerged not a pack of rangers but a single ranger. The mayor, she said, asked where the other rangers were. To which, Officer Jordan recited, the lone ranger replied, "Ain't I enough? You only got one prize fight."

"Poor Rangers," Officer Jordan said, "always outnumbered by the lawless." To The Serial Stowaway, Officer Jordan's braids seemed to float.

Now the star, Officer Jordan continued, then stopped. "That star. The one Clint wears isn't part of our uniform. It's a Texas Ranger star he bought off the internet or when he visited the Texas Ranger museum. He ditches it whenever the big bosses come around. Clint's named after the Texas Ranger who broke up La Grange Chicken Ranch—that's a brothel. That star he wears is harmless." She took a sip of Arizona iced tea. "That star there on that guy's shirt," she gestured with her can toward the lobby, "that one not so much."

That figure in the statue, she explained, was a Texas

Ranger named Jay Banks. "His name's not on there, but that's who it is." Ranger Jay Banks was head of the Rangers squad brought in by the governor when a court ordered integration of a high school thirty miles from Dallas. Whites were rioting, and the governor told the Rangers to keep the Black kids out of the white school. Which is exactly what happened. The town's White Citizens Council rewarded Banks with a chicken dinner.

"There's some beautiful photographs of Ranger Banks from that time," the officer said. "Let's see, there's Banks leaning against a tree in front of the high school, looking about as bothered as he looks in that statue, with a blackface dummy hanging from a noose behind him. Then there's the photograph of Banks standing next to a guy holding a sign that says, 'Niggers stay out.'"

Officer Jordan asked The Serial Stowaway if she minded staying outdoors a while, despite the noise and heat, and The Serial Stowaway said that would be fine, and Officer Jordan said they had more time before the flight before she said nothing for a while.

Finally, she spoke again, possibly to herself. "There's another motto for the Texas Rangers," she said, "It goes, 'Little man whip a big man every time if the little man's in the right and he keeps a-coming.'" They were both silent a moment.

"Now that's a sneaky motto," Officer Jordan said. "That's a motto with some prettiness, like a handsome man with charm. You hear that motto, and you don't think how fundamentally stupid it is. At no time and in no way is a Texas Ranger ever a little man, and at no time and in no way is he ever fighting a big man. Sorry, pal. Other way around. Still, you hear that motto and you think, maybe *I'm* the little man. Maybe I'm the one in the right. Maybe I'm the one who just keeps a-coming. And so, when you think about Texas Rangers you feel a little hope, like maybe you have a little, I don't know, a little power, and there's going to be a little justice. But then if you stop a minute, if you think about it a minute, it kind of falls apart. I'm not a man. I'm tired of keeping a-coming. And I don't notice any whipping of any big men. More the opposite. And less like whipping and more like killing."

Officer Jordan's lips showed signs of shifting expression, although The Serial Stowaway could not tell whether toward smile or sneer. A bus passed, and to The Serial Stowaway its exhaust seemed to wipe the scene away. Officer Jordan tipped her head back for the last of the Arizona Iced Tea. "Well, little woman," she said, "time for you to keep a-coming." She withdrew from her pocket her lanyard and ID badge in preparation for getting The Serial Stowaway past yet another checkpoint.

Chapter 4:
The Serial Stowaway and the Hawaiian Experience

When her mother died at age eighty-one, The Serial Stowaway, then fifty-seven, left her longtime job as a law-firm receptionist. At that job she was snapped at on the telephone by clients who could not be immediately connected to their attorneys and by prospective clients who were not allowed to tell their troubles immediately to an attorney and by callers for no discernible reason and by attorneys in the firm who did not want to speak to current clients and by attorneys who did not want to speak to prospective clients and by attorneys for no apparent reason. Sometimes, the prospective and current clients, unsuccessful in getting an attorney on the phone, would narrate their stories to The Serial Stowaway—from the genesis of their predicaments all the way up to the critical moments that precipitated this phone call. The attorneys, to a person saying they did not have time to speak to these people on the phone, would later spend serious swaths of time telling their clients' stories to The Serial Stowaway, with more levity and less angst but an equivalent amount of swearing compared to the clients' versions. None of which particularly bothered The Serial Stowaway.

When the attorneys found out that The Serial Stowaway was resigning, they stopped talking to her, except for one, just out of law school, who asked The Serial Stowaway why she was resigning and then, without waiting for a response, said, "I guess it was just time, huh?"

The Serial Stowaway calculated that the payout from her mother's tiny life insurance policy would allow her to subsist until she could receive her monthly Social Security benefit, which she calculated would allow her something shy of subsistence thereafter. She moved into a three-story senior-living complex named Library Towers on Library Lane in Libertyville, Illinois, the village hall of which was 36 miles north of the Chicago City Hall.

Her finances and housing settled, The Serial Stowaway began riding trains.

From Library Towers, The Serial Stowaway could walk to the Libertyville train station in eight minutes on a bright day and in eleven minutes on a blustery day. For thirty dollars per month, The Serial Stowaway purchased a transit pass. With that pass, she rode the Milwaukee District north line for one hour and sixteen minutes to Union Station in Chicago. There she would sit on the long wooden pews in the high-ceiling atrium and stroll slowly through the erratically laid-out corridors while streams of fast-walking commuters fast-walked around her.

Other days, from Union Station she rode the North Central Service Line for thirty-four minutes to the O'Hare Airport transit center, from there taking the Airport Transit Shuttle to one of the four terminals, where she would sit in one of the few banks of seats available before entering security.

The Serial Stowaway enjoyed her time sitting and wandering in Union Station and O'Hare Airport. She also enjoyed waiting for her trains in the Libertyville Metra station—she never timed her arrival for a particular scheduled train, instead simply showing up when she showed up and waiting. What she enjoyed most of all, however, was the time between her points of origin and her termini.

She imagined herself traveling within the handle of a huge, elongated dumbbell, the rounded heads providing a place to comfortably turn around and return to the path connecting the ends. On that path, seated on the Metra train, she felt endlessly entertained by the humming, sometimes rocking, sometimes lurching steel compartment. She rarely looked out the windows. She wasn't particularly aware of looking at anything. She simply sat and enjoyed the vibrations and sounds and passage of time. There was nothing else she needed to do; there was nothing else she could do. She was simply *here*.

Her only complaint about these trips was that they didn't last long enough. Seventy-six minutes from Libertyville to Union Station or thirty-four minutes to O'Hare felt like she was only getting started. This couldn't truly be called dissatisfaction. These were the trips available to The Serial Stowaway through her thirty-dollar monthly pass. They were good trips. She was content with extending them simply by repeating them. She felt no need to permeate the termini, to break through the heads of the dumbbells in search of other trips.

Once The Serial Stowaway transitioned from legitimate Chicago-area train rides to illegitimate domestic and international airplane rides, that propensity to not permeate her termini continued. In Paris, she did not leave the airport to see the Eiffel Tower or the Louvre, and in Stockholm, she did not leave the airport to see the Royal Palace or ABBA The Museum. Part of that was pragmatic; were she to exit through security, she would have to sneak back through security, and although that was something she had proven she could accomplish, it was an effort not necessary. Not to her, at any rate, because any compulsion to explore felt by The Serial Stowaway ended, at least at the beginning, when she reached each flight's destination.

The Serial Stowaway's recent excursion outside Dallas Love Field, Bruegger's Bagel sandwiches in hand, accompanied by Officer Charline Jordan, did nothing to change her habits, the humidity and gritty air and noise being far less desirable than the airport ambience.

Perhaps it was inevitable that The Serial Stowaway would eventually break free of airports, would eventually explore one of the cities, glorious and otherwise, to which she traveled. But whether that breaking free was due to a desire to explore, a convergence of unforeseen circumstances, or some cause that resists explanation is—like so many things about The Serial Stowaway—hard to say. What we can say is that the city into which she finally transported herself in a non-airplane manner was the lush city sometimes called The Big Pineapple: Honolulu, Hawaii.

On the flight from Chicago to Honolulu, The Serial Stowaway had a vague sense of more attention directed toward her by one flight attendant than the others. This attendant, oddly, appeared to be older than The Serial Stowaway, although professionally groomed and with the presence of an actor in a musical comedy just before breaking into song. However, any unpleasantness resulting from this attendant's possible curiosity toward The Serial Stowaway was thwarted when, as the passengers began to deplane, one cried out a discovery: that this flight attendant was not just a flight attendant, but also played the role of Esther Valentine on the television soap opera titled "The Young and The Restless," a role she had begun 38 years before and continued to play, taping the show on weekdays and serving as a flight attendant on weekends. The passengers who lingered, others grunting as they edged past, knew only the actor's character name, but the actor did not seem to mind, supplying her real name when asked: Kate Linder. Passing the cluster of people surrounding the actor, The Serial Stowaway heard her say, "I don't believe in retirement. As long as I can do both jobs, and do them well, I will keep doing them."

In general, The Serial Stowaway didn't mind long flights. However, the flight to Honolulu was even longer than her flights to Paris and almost as long as her flight to Stockholm. True, she had been entertained by a man with a brush-like white mustache that seemed to hover above his words and fluttering fingers that seemed to give wings to his words who had explained how he had invented modern logistics, first for the U.S. Army and then for Walmart. The man was in the aisle seat, The Serial Stowaway was as usual in the middle seat, and in the window seat sat a woman about the same age as the logistics expert who dozed or looked toward the window with the most perfect expression of contentment and no engagement whatsoever, verbal or visual or apparently auditory, in the exchange between the logistics expert and The Serial Stowaway.

According to the man's explanation, as best The Serial Stowaway could discern over aircraft noise, his invention involved supply warehouses located within computer-calculatedly efficient distances of the sites that used the supplies. The warehouses stocked computer-calculated amounts of frequently needed supplies, robots picked supplies based on standing or one-time orders from stock, and the supplies were sent by specially designed vehicles—perhaps driven by robots, The Serial Stowaway was fuzzy on that—to the requesting facility, whether army outpost or Walmart Superstore. All in all, the system didn't seem terribly special to The Serial Stowaway, reminding her as it did of every airport she had ever been to, if you substituted terminal for warehouse, airplane for site of use, and passengers for supplies. Even more familiar about the scheme was its similarity to The Serial Stowaway's dumbbell-shaped train travel. What the scheme lacked in originality, it made up for in the feeling of comfort for The Serial Stowaway from its familiar design and the logistics man's fluttering fingers.

As hours passed and the man continued his discourse, now broadened to include executive teams and boards that had foolishly questioned the need to invest in his scheme and been proved wrong, a question began to tickle The Serial Stowaway. At about the four-hour mark in the man's discourse, when the man took a sip of Diet Coke, the question emerged, as if unbidden, from her lips. "You are a man of great knowledge," she started, setting up the question, and the man, in mid-swallow, nodded soberly. "How," The Serial Stowaway continued, "can a person gain as much knowledge as you have gained without ever pausing long enough to consume some of that knowledge from others?" She surprised herself at how biblical her question sounded.

The man laughed, smiled like an angel, and said, his mustache floating and his fingers fluttering, "Oh, I didn't learn anything from anyone. I invented all this myself."

When the flight landed, the man stepped out of his seat and gestured for The Serial Stowaway to precede him. Waiting for the line in the aisle to move, The Serial Stowaway looked back and saw the woman from the window seat standing next to the logistics man, squeezing his arm.

In no hurry to scout for a flight home, The Serial Stowaway ventured into the corridors of the building, which according to a framed poster with a photograph of the ceremony, had recently been rechristened the Daniel K. Inouye International Airport.

Next to the poster of the christening was a map in which

the layout of the Daniel K. Inouye International Airport resembled the Eiffel Tower, making The Serial Stowaway wish she had left the airport in Paris to see it. A narrow strip at the map's top was labeled as containing ten gates, a flower shop, a lei kiosk, two gift shops both called Hawaiian Isle Memories (separated by a newsstand) and another gift shop across the corridor called Take Home the Aloha, a snack shop called The Hawaiian Market, and finally a Starbucks. This narrow strip gave way to what looked like the broad base of the tower, which the map depicted as large, empty, and strikingly green, although no labels suggested what this large green space contained.

For the moment, the large green space being both unknown and probably beyond a TSA checkpoint, The Serial Stowaway opted to stay within the portion of the terminal in the map's narrow strip. She draped around her neck a free lei from the kiosk and sat in a bench that was shaped like a ladle near the newsstand, where she ate a tuna jerky sampler she had stolen from the Hawaiian Market. Then she slumped into the ladle and dozed.

When she awoke, it was still light, but with a late-afternoon quality. Shaking off sleep, The Serial Stowaway ambled past the ten gates of the concourse, discovering that the last direct flight back to Chicago was boarding, and the crowd at the gate suggested a full flight.

It was not in The Serial Stowaway's nature to feel disappointment. What was in The Serial Stowaway's nature was to invite fortune and to not presume which sort of fortune it would be. With no possibility of flying home that day, her invitation to fortune was to head toward the end of the area depicted on the airport map by a narrow strip, the area well-populated by familiar things, and to venture toward that space on the map shown as large, green, and unlabeled, the space that resembled the base of the Eiffel Tower.

At what seemed the border to this unknown place, The Serial Stowaway faced a battery of doors, all closed. Pushing against the crash bar of one, she opened it and, although she had not passed security and thus logically was still within the airport, found herself outside.

The air was on the cool side of warm, and moist, with a few shallow puddles dotting a concrete-paved patio; apparently, it had rained while she had dozed. Along the patio was a glass-enclosed conference center; she could see through some of the windows what looked like chairs that would be rated quite well using the conference-chair-rating system she had finalized just before her interrogation in the Dallas Love Field conference room.

The patio held a few widely spaced food kiosks: Burger King, Chow Mein Express, and California Pizza Kitchen. However, overwhelming this thinness of food options was the richness, the denseness, the greenness of the sight below: a tapestry of green leaves, the green made even more potent by the contrasting spots of bright color within, stretching if not as far as the eye could see—at the borders were car tops peeking over overpasses—far enough for The Serial Stowaway to feel a swimming sensation that she was not sure was entirely pleasant.

She pushed the mild unpleasantness aside, recognizing

her current setting as good fortune: an opportunity for fresh air, an opportunity to experience Hawaii, and an opportunity for the revolution of exploration outside a terminus without technically permeating its borders.

Descending a staircase, The Serial Stowaway emerged into something that neither the green block on the map nor the tapestry image from above had led her to expect. To The Serial Stowaway's right was a plaque. Alas, she was too distracted to read it. The plaque, a rather wordy one, read as follows:

> Serenity is found in the Japanese Garden. Across a zigzag bridge (which keeps away evil) is a wood shingle-roofed shelter with stone benches. Colorful carp fish create patterns in the ponds surrounded by sculptured pine and weeping willow trees. Stone lanterns softly illuminate the setting at dusk. A commemorative pagoda on an elevated plateau at one end was donated by Hawaii's Japanese community on the Centennial Anniversary of the first Japanese immigrants to Hawaii.

Having not received these instructions on how to react to this scene, The Serial Stowaway, like a viewer of a film without a musical accompaniment, was left to emotional reaction based solely on her own perceptions and proclivities. Rather than the elegant pattern of a tapestry she had viewed from above, what The Serial Stowaway had been dropped into she could only perceive as a chaos of disconnected, well, *things*. Things pointing one way, things pointing another way. Things in one shape, things in another shape. Things taller and things shorter. Things all green and therefore difficult to distinguish from one another. Small bursts of color that were like people jumping out of doorways and saying, "Boo!" Paths, yes, paths, but paths that did not extend in any way The Serial Stowaway could see, but that disappeared around corners and reappeared in the distance. Smells that bumped into one another. Sounds of insects and birds and water and, at precisely the same volume, distant traffic. The things tallied as kineticism surpassing the Union Station lobby where The Serial Stowaway once spent her afternoons as a contented rock in a rapids of people.

Before taking her next steps, The Serial Stowaway tapped her foot ahead as if testing the soundness of the earth, not from fear but only the good sense of trying to avoid stepping on something dangerous, such as a trap door, in this chaos. In this manner, The Serial Stowaway felt her way onto and along a path, scanning her surroundings for something around which she might order the disorder surrounding her. Here, as was so often The Serial Stowaway's lot, she met with success. In the distance she saw bursting forth above the chaos of green, a pagoda—the one described so eloquently on the plaque that The Serial Stowaway had not seen.

The pagoda's height gave The Serial Stowaway a north star. Unfortunately, it's all well and good to have a north star, but when the path under your feet zigs and zags to ward off evil, the path can also ward off reaching one's destination, no matter how well one can see it.

The Serial Stowaway persisted, and around one zig, or perhaps it was a zag, she found herself stepping onto a bridge over a koi pond, and across that bridge she saw not the pagoda, but, she reflected, perhaps something just as good. It was not a glamorous structure, to be sure. At its top was a limp-looking wood-thatched circular roof. The roof hovered over a circular concrete floor, on which stood a circular concrete table around which were concrete cylinders. The cylinders might have registered to The Serial Stowaway as design elements rather than stools had one not been occupied.

As The Serial Stowaway approached, the person on the concrete stool became not so much a person as the human embodiment of the Japanese Garden: dark hair that evoked artful chaos surrounding the contrasting pop of a pale, angular face and eyes. On the table were spread a quantity of supplies great enough to nearly overwhelm the human they served: a leather-trimmed canvas portfolio, an open laptop computer, a large but sleek smartphone, a pad of drawing paper, a tray of colored pens, a paper coffee cup, a plastic bowl mostly full of noodles, and chopsticks. Next to the table was a pristine, compact navy rolling suitcase, handle extended.

Accustomed to close-proximity seating, The Serial Stowaway stepped onto the slab and started toward one of the cylindrical stools, at which point the woman seated on a cylinder on the slab in the shelter, smartphone poised over a page in the sketch pad, turned her head toward The Serial Stowaway and said with a combination of enthusiasm and matter-of-factness, "Thank, goodness. Come. Sit."

The Serial Stowaway did, on the stool to which the woman gestured with her free hand, the phone retaining its position.

"This is just impossible," the woman said. "Every shot I take the shadow of the phone covers half the image. It looks so amateurish, and no one will be able to read the words." She paused. "Although that may be a good thing," she said, and rolled her eyes.

Surveying The Serial Stowaway, who happened to be looking toward the bowl of noodles, the woman said, "Please tell me you're hungry. I can't begin to finish this, and I hate wasting food. Have you ever been to Hawaii? This is my first time. The sign at the market said this is traditional Hawaiian comfort food, I think it's called Saimin, and good lord I need comfort, but I'm getting stuffed beyond comfort."

She pushed the plastic bowl toward The Serial Stowaway, who picked up the chopsticks and fished out noodles while the woman silently continued attempting shots from different angles of the sheet in her sketch pad.

When The Serial Stowaway put down the chopsticks, the woman spoke. "Done? Good. Was it good? I liked it. Now, I'm sorry, but can you help me for a sec? I don't mean to impose. Were you planning to sit here for a sec? It's just, look, would you hold this up?" She proffered the sketchbook toward The Serial Stowaway, who took it. "Not like hold it up in the air, you can let the bottom rest on the table, I think, just kind of hold it upright. I just, can we just try a few angles? I just want to get rid of that darned camera shadow, and if I can get the garden kind of peeking around the corner, that would be perfect."

The woman looked at her phone screen as the camera looked at the sketchbook and the garden in the background.

After various permutations of camera and sketchbook angles, the woman declared, "Yep, there," and The Serial Stowaway held her position. "It's for my Insta story," she said. As though the thought were connected with the previous one, she continued, "I've been journaling like crazy."

Proceeding to take pictures of pages from the sketchpad propped up by The Serial Stowaway, the woman said, "I think I'm nervous about this conference. I mean, not about the conference, that's my business, I put on meetings sort of like this one, although not in Hawaii, but anyway this will be great, it's my tribe, so much support, but I really am hoping to get some venture funding. No, that's me understating things as usual. I am not *hoping* to get venture funding, I *need* venture funding. So, I need to show up with a clear head. So, you know," she gestured with her chin toward the sketchpad, "journaling."

From her position to one side of the sketchpad, The Serial Stowaway regarded what the successive sheets revealed. Each sheet was crowded, top to bottom, side to side, with thin-lined words of multiple colors—huge headlines, smaller text, colors shifting each sentence from purple to blue to orange to red. The handwriting had the care of an adult but the shape of a much younger person, even a teenager, that sense reinforced by the occasional bursts of tiny hearts floating where the words did not completely fill the page and a single tiny heart at the end of each journal entry.

What The Serial Stowaway read was this:

Healing Housing

It can all be abundant at the same time. Your platform is being rebuilt beneath your feet as you cry on the plane. Just the first step. And it's ok for the next step to look like this. It doesn't mean anything about your future reality that isn't so far away from now. The passage of time is scary, but just like money—time is something we invented. You can stay in love in the present, and in the flow. Things are moving towards you. Keep believing.

Freedom

It comes with a cost, unfortunately. Michelle said: So many women never get to be free: and sadly she's right now...but I have hope. It's truly the only currency I know how to manage. (lol)

1 in 4 women in the U.S. will experience intimate partner violence, making it a serious public health issue. (Mass General Brigham McLean Hospital)

Everyone deserves space to heal, and we have plenty of room. We have what we need to change these stats. In America, we believe in freedom so let's build a future where we can all be more free. Send in the calvary, let the healers heal. Let us all be free.

Ballerinas

Let us dance in your dreams and in your hearts. To move is a gift and a biological need...to find our rhythm in order to soothe...in order to heal. "She's always twirling" is what my mother always said. She repeats the same stories again and again to try to hold on to the memories and keep hold while her mind is slipping away, her body keeping her sick and scared. She was afraid all her life, but she

knew how to stay graceful, floating in public and crum-
bling behind closed doors, but on the stage of life we
must perform. For her and for me and for all of us, I wish
rest, ease and peace. The ballerinas in the future won't
push so hard. They will glide, and dance, and explore
what freedom can feel like.

Hiding

While so much of me has been exposed, an open wound,
running from the river to my coffee shop shooting ar-
rows in the sky and setting off flares for someone to spy
in the open sky, the boat I was floating in was gently eas-
ing into a dock that I couldn't see because of the fog.
There was no way for me to know this harbor would be
open, so I burned all my fuel (and then some) on the way
to where I am today. I have no regrets but do feel periods
of shame and guilt for mistakes I made while hiding in
terror from monsters both real and imaginary. And yet I
haven't been exposed in the ways that I feared I was.
They have seen me struggle and survive, the darling girls
inside women's bodies who have been hiding and hurt-
ing, too. We are finding each other with open arms.

Just ok

When you're grieving some days will be just ok. Some
will be harder than you can impossibly imagine, and some
will surprise—scare you with how whole you can feel
again. But in the dark dense moments, someone always
shows up to remind you that you are going to be ok again.
Maybe it's a kind man with a white dog with brown spots,
and a group chat with smart women, and a Brazilian

mom, and a lunch date with my boys. You've been re-building, finding what you need, falling and being caught by a goddess or a gift, something completely out of your control. Your habits and safe spaces give you comfort, and they see your highs and lows, and when you can, on days like today, even when you are just ok, you can smile again. Don't brace for the next wave. You are ok.

TROLLS

They live under bridges? Nah. I've seen plenty walking into houses in the best parts of town. Men who own things. They sit in coffee shops reading the paper, pre-tending to understand the articles, drooling over girls in cute outfits, knowing…they can pay for her attention. As long as she has less. Or as long as the danger of being seen as "rude" in the eyes—on the lips—of a powerful man exists. She must politely decline even if her financial net worth is equal or higher. Our financial superiority is coming. It's here: ask Taylor. That is why the trolls have taken over our government towers (shoot them down). To lay down laws to make us obey even when we earn more. When the word of a man is true because he spoke first, you live in Virginia, Missouri, Arizona, etc., etc. How do we banish the trolls?

Heaven

(A poem for a boy that I met at a club. A long time ago….Like, in a past life….)

I sleep just fine. Heaven is an orgasm in a bathtub with a man named XXX. Everything is alright when he calls me back. Take my breath away. Put your fingers in so deep that blood flows and stains your sheets because nothing matters. Why would I kill for one more night bent over your bed? No one will ever understand my desire for you.

Not even you! But in my daydreams I fuck you ten times a day and orgasm on my own on a towel on the floor of a hotel room in Miami. I took a walk in the city to clear my head and looked for you. But you left me behind. This is breakup poetry for a man who never liked me back. He is a sign; something I want? a lesson? a message? I think of him. He fills my pages. He triggers my fear. He gives me nothing, but my thoughts are filled. I'm filled up. All the way. Like the one night he chose me. He fucked me. He growled at me. Lifted me higher than I'd been before. I'm sure he was high though. (lol) Will I ever be fucked that good again? If not, what's the fucking point? Living on Earth is boring. It's strange that these memories are still so clear. This happened before "it" happened. Still so clear. Before my most recent death. Why when I was killed did I not get sent back...to heaven?

LOCKED UP

It wasn't an illusion. You were a prisoner of war. You still are. They cover your hair, they empty your womb and try to fill it again. The closest you came to Utopia was freezing cold. His skin like ice against you in a black room where you couldn't see. Before the lockdown that stole all the lies you were very good at believing to save you from ending it all. Women have been and are being beaten in the streets, locked in cages, and left to fend for themselves in alleys like dogs. And you turn away, shield your eyes, pretend to believe a crate is a place any bitch wants to be. I wasn't tossed out, I was released. Those who hunted me beware. When I rise again there will be hurricanes of fire.

Magic

is everywhere.
—in castles
—Pinterest
—smiles from a stranger
—on the dance floor
—inside closets
—on the backs of raindrops
Ladybugs
Rainbows
Twin lions
Dolphins
White birds
Cardinals
White dogs w/ brown spots
Every time you jump you land back on the ground. Ideas keep finding you. Support put in your path. It's hard to trust but you keep trusting. Somehow you always know the next step. You resolve mistakes that seem overwhelming—
WHEN you LET GO!!

This one was in two columns, with drawings of a sun with broad rays, multiple ladybugs, a row of green hearts before the last line, and a smiley face after.

"That last one is old," the woman said, "but I just had to pull it out today."

While the woman, positioning herself so the foliage was visible behind her, narrated a short video into her phone, The Serial Stowaway stood, nodded her thanks and walked back across the bridge.

Those who saw the woman's Instagram story in the

twenty-four hours it was available, on which her journal entries were posted, saw, in the quick introductory video, something even quicker: a fleeting glimpse in the frame's upper right corner of the face of The Serial Stowaway bearing a thoughtful expression.

The Serial Stowaway was not able to retrace the path she had taken to the shelter but cobbled together something that took her to the stairs toward the concrete terrace and the battery of doors into the airport. Inside, walking two clockwise and three counterclockwise circuits of the small main terminal, The Serial Stowaway considered the journal pages she had helped photograph. They were pretty. So colorful. So carefully lettered. So large—significantly larger than the copy paper at the law firm, and cream-colored rather than bright white, and richly textured rather than smooth. The Serial Stowaway had never seen anyone's journal—not surprising, she thought, because as she understood these things, journals were private—and she had never kept a journal herself, but if anyone had asked her to describe the text of a journal, she would have guessed dark with crabbed, black-inked handwriting. As pretty as this journal was, it did raise a few questions for The Serial Stowaway.

The most obvious question—why the woman would make public her highly personal journal—The Serial Stowaway dismissed quickly. That was the woman's lookout, and surely she had calculated the debits and credits in much the way The Serial Stowaway did with her gambits for getting past airport security and gate attendants. Another question was who the people named in the journal—Michelle and Taylor—were. In the context of the journal, they seemed knowledgeable and worth knowing. The Serial Stowaway also wondered why, in the entry titled "Heaven," if the woman had sex with the boy ten times each day, the woman had her orgasm in private, in the hotel bathroom. Perhaps that was exactly the way these things worked, even in a heavenly experience. However, the entry was labeled as a poem, and the passage a fantasy, so perhaps it was not intended to be realistic, although The Serial Stowaway had her doubts.

The Serial Stowaway liked the entry called "Healing Housing." It reminded The Serial Stowaway of her apartment in the Library Towers in Libertyville. She missed her apartment on evenings like this—for the sun had set by now—when she could not return to it. She would not have thought of that word "healing" for her home because she wasn't sick, but she of course recognized that healing was a good thing and having a home was a good thing, so she liked the way the woman put two good things together in this part of her journal.

The entry that The Serial Stowaway liked best was the one called "Freedom," mostly because it contained facts and numbers, which gave a sense of certainty. The woman used that word "healing" again, which didn't connect very clearly with freedom, but it was obviously one of the woman's favorite words, and The Serial Stowaway guessed that everyone had favorite words, although she wasn't sure which hers were.

Speaking of putting words together, The Serial Stowaway

liked the way the woman put "hurricane" and "fire" together, although the combination was a little frightening.

At the far end of the concourse, The Serial Stowaway found another ladle-shaped seat and perched on its rim. She reviewed her day. She had thought about permeating the boundaries of the airport. She had thought that the Japanese Garden was a way to do that, a safe way, a way that would not actually leave the airport, but would seem as if she had. But the Japanese Garden had not been terribly pleasant, although she had gotten the nice meal from the woman with the journal, and she had learned that it was difficult to take a picture with a phone of a piece of paper without getting the phone's shadow in the picture.

The Serial Stowaway slumped within the ladle-shaped seat. Just before she fell asleep, something cloudy entered her mood, something like the unusual, for her, sensation of disappointment.

Who is to say why what happened next happened? Perhaps the cause was her dream image: a schoolchild-quality colored-pencil drawing of a gigantic wave approaching a beach, the wave's ridge decorated with flames. Perhaps during sleep, The Serial Stowaway's vague sense of disappointment grew in intensity and gained the focus of a clear action that would bring about its relief. Perhaps The Serial Stowaway was not fond of the standing sign she saw when she opened her eyes, which featured a cartoonish illustration of a not-erupting volcano surrounded by palm trees. Perhaps she was reacting to the one a.m. quality of the darkness she saw through the windows, letting her know that she had many hours still to pass before the next flight. Perhaps she was even considering staying in Honolulu and simply wanted to scout the city before making her decision.

Whatever the reason, for the first time in her travels, The Serial Stowaway passed the security checkpoint in egress, feeling exhilarated by the freedom to legitimately stride past the guard, only one guard, almost asleep but awake enough to give, from his seated position, a Buddhist bow to The Serial Stowaway.

From this point of liberation, she crossed to a set of doors, which opened automatically, and, easy as that, she was outside—not in the Japanese Garden, but really and truly outside.

Had The Serial Stowaway been another sort of person, the enormity of her task would have been apparent within only a few steps. However, The Serial Stowaway was not the sort of person to assess her tasks, but one to perform her tasks, and so she walked. She walked on the sidewalk. When the sidewalk petered out, she walked on the dirt beside the road. When vegetation crowded her, she walked on the road. She walked under one large directional sign hanging over the road and was approaching a second when a car distinguishable as a police car passed her on the left and seconds later, presumably having made a U-turn, slowed beside her, angled to block her path, and stopped, emitting two officers, both of whom shone flashlights first at The Serial Stowaway's face, and then, when she shielded her eyes, toward her feet. In this light, the officers appeared as hazy silhouettes.

When one officer asked The Serial Stowaway where she

was headed, she told him she was headed to Honolulu to visit her cousin. The other officer, as best The Serial Stowaway could tell in this odd light, cocked his head.

When the speaking officer told The Serial Stowaway that the walk would take her two hours—doable, but not a great idea alone at (he shone his flashlight on his wristwatch) one-twenty a.m., especially because much of the route did not have sidewalks, and rain was in the forecast, she said, oh, she had meant to say she was on her way to the airport to take a plane to visit her sister. The nonspeaking officer cocked his head in the other direction.

When the speaking officer told The Serial Stowaway that if that were the case, she was headed in the wrong direction and asked to see her identification, she told the officer she had none. The other officer nodded.

When the speaking officer asked if she had any money, The Serial Stowaway consulted the hip pockets of her slacks and reported she had four dollars and thirty-one cents. The other officer shook his head.

When the speaking officer said that was not enough money to buy an airplane ticket, The Serial Stowaway said that perhaps after all she should go to Honolulu and take a bus to see her cousin. The other officer shrugged. The speaking officer shrugged. And they gave her a ride to the bus station in downtown Honolulu, outside of which was a white rectangle with the words Aloha The Bus.

There, sitting beside a woman accompanied by a white dog with brown spots, The Serial Stowaway felt the satisfaction of a task completed. She had permeated a terminus; she had broken through the head of the dumbbell. She had seen a new place—not an airport, but a city, the lush, tropical city of Honolulu. She looked once more at the white dog with brown spots, let her eyes close, and decided that the woman in the Japanese Garden was right. Magic was everywhere, although The Serial Stowaway was not, herself, fond of lady-bugs.

Chapter 5:
The Serial Stowaway
and the Professional Protester

Inside the airplane scheduled to fly from Chicago to Washington, D.C., every seat in the first half of the fuselage was taken, and the overhead storage compartments showed barely a sliver of space, but after that, the seating opened up quite a bit. In one way, this was good for The Serial Stowaway. On underpopulated flights, it was less likely that another passenger would appear at the last minute with a boarding pass bearing the row and seat she had chosen to occupy, and if one did appear, she would be able to feign a mistake and move to another open seat. On the other hand, the basic arithmetic of a less-full flight worked in The Serial Stowaway's disfavor, creating a higher stowaway-to-non-stowaway ratio, making it more likely that an attendant would have the capacity to spot and confront an interloper.

The Serial Stowaway had ventured into the meagerly populated half of the airplane, decided to treat herself with the window seat in a two-seat row (her usual selection being the undesirable middle-seat of a three-seat row), and had turned to slide into the seat as most people do, back toward seat back, front toward airplane front, when her attention was drawn to a contretemps.

A firm-jawed female flight attendant was facing off against a put-upon-looking young male in a track suit standing in front of a full overhead storage compartment. The flight attendant, who had wonderfully broad shoulders, wonderfully broad hair, and a uniform distinct from that of the other flight attendants, suggesting a higher rank, was pointing toward the contents of the compartment and, in an I-tried-asking-and-now-I'm-ordering tone of voice, told the young man that the overhead compartment was for suitcases and he was to remove his backpack and put it under the seat, and he was to do it now.

The young man, a half-head taller than the attendant, set his shoulders as if ready to continue his non-capitulation indefinitely. The attendant, her every feature indicating she had no time for a standoff with this insignificant person, grabbed the backpack's strap and began tugging it from the compartment. The young man lurched into action, pulling the backpack, which turned out to be quite plump, from the compartment. With a snort and a pout, he plopped into his seat and began stuffing the backpack under the seat in front, the size of the backpack making the task resemble a Saturday-morning cartoon scene that The Serial Stowaway recalled of an elephant being stuffed into a mousehole. The attendant marched off before the young man's effort was complete.

Seeing that he was now unobserved by a personage more

imposing than himself, the young man yanked the backpack out—The Serial Stowaway fancied she heard a pop—and, standing, took one more glance to confirm his nemesis was not watching, and began stuffing the backpack into its previous place in the overhead storage compartment.

The man had not yet completed the stuffing when The Serial Stowaway reached his side, said, "That's all right, dear, I'll put that under my own seat," reached up, with surprising strength plucked out the backpack (the pop again sounding in her mind), and, cradling the backpack in her arms, returned to her seat, leaving the young man, still standing next to the open overhead bin, looking as if he had lost a bet he did not remember having made. At her seat, The Serial Stowaway quickly removed three protein bars from the backpack, and, with unaccountably less difficulty than the young man had experienced, put the pack under the seat in front of her.

Reclining into the seatback, The Serial Stowaway allowed her eyes to drift toward the window through which she was reasonably sure she saw a shirtless man—surely he was chilly on this March morning—strolling past the workers lifting luggage from a carrier next to the plane. She was watching the man wave at the workers when she was distracted by her seat being bumped—once, twice, thrice. Or were they not three bumps but three bounces? Either or both, they served admirably as *les trois coups* to announce the commencement of the drama to come.

Someone was depositing himself in the aisle seat beside her. Although this action was a simple one, for this man it

seemed to involve multiple movements in different directions simultaneously, which he accomplished energetically,
extemporaneously, but harmoniously. On his head was a
straw hat, on his nose wire-rimmed glasses, around his neck
a narrow brown tie, and on his lap, a well-worn and sizable
soft leather briefcase as creased as the man's face, although
The Serial Stowaway calculated his age at no more than forty-
five. In contrast to his trappings of studiousness, the man
seemed potently athletic—lean and tall. Also, revealed when
he briefly removed his hat, his mostly bald head was shaped
like a bullet.

The man leaned forward to stuff his briefcase under the
seat in front of him, reappeared, turned toward The Serial
Stowaway, and said, waving his boarding pass, "This isn't my
assigned seat, but fuck seat assignments. I want to sit next to
you." He paused. "If that's OK?"

He waited, focused on The Serial Stowaway as if poised
to hear from an oracle. She nodded.

He nodded, dropped his voice, and said, "I saw what you
did there." Smiling hugely, voice still low, he said, "Badass."

Soon, the announcements about flight safety completed,
the attendant, the one who had had the kerfuffle with the
young man, came into The Serial Stowaway's field of vision,
briskly checking seated passengers against a list in her left
hand. In her peripheral vision, The Serial Stowaway saw that
the man next to her had registered the same happening. As
was her practice at this stage of her many flights, The Serial
Stowaway commenced to become invisible. She made her
breathing shallow. She slowed her heartbeat. Her vision

blurred. She felt herself become smaller. She felt herself become translucent. For all the times The Serial Stowaway had carried out this practice, this was the first flight during which she was aware that her seatmate was doing the same. When the attendant had passed, both inhaled and straightened up.

After the plane had taken off, the man, his straw hat becoming askew, fished out his briefcase and from that fished out what looked to The Serial Stowaway like two worn manila folders, a yellow legal pad, and a ballpoint pen with a colorful exterior. Straightening his hat, lowering his tray, and opening one of the folders, the man began to read what looked like a document with a legal heading of the sort The Serial Stowaway had, although only a receptionist, seen at the legal office where she had worked for so many years. With the pen, which The Serial Stowaway now saw was decorated with an undulating and rather sophisticated reproduction of the American flag's stars and stripes, the man began making firm underlines and heartfelt marginal notes.

Not many minutes into his work, the man took out his pad of paper and slid the legal document to one side on the insufficient surface of the tray table.

The Serial Stowaway asked, "Are you an attorney?"

The man looked at her and paused as if making a decision. "Pro se attorney," he said. "I represent myself." He rested the pen on top of the document.

"That's a nice pen," The Serial Stowaway said, surprising herself with her conversational initiative. But it was a nice pen. Very sophisticated design. The finish looked like satin.

The man seemed pleased. "A gift from my friends at the

Library of Congress."

"Is that where you work?"

"I suppose I do. They've given me some paid, part-time duties. Helping others with research, a little filing. But I'm there all day anyway. Except for my mornings at the Capitol."

They were silent then. The Serial Stowaway listened to the airplane throb, and she told herself that the man, his eyes now closed, was doing the same. Eventually, the man opened his eyes, leaned around his tray, and, holding his straw hat in place, rooted around in his briefcase, while resuming the conversation. "What I am," he said, "I'm what's called a professional protester, although the 'professional' part is absurd, because I'm not being paid." He emerged with a folder. "But people make words mean what they want them to mean to suit their purposes," he said while opening the folder and pointing to the sheet of paper on top. "I've settled on handing out seventeen pieces of paper cut into three pieces— that's fifty-one handouts, which takes me through a morning rush."

The pages seemed to be divided into three horizontal strips with roughly the same handwriting on each. The man picked up the pages and flipped through them, revealing similar ones in the stack, but too rapidly for The Serial Stowaway to see much more than "C.I.A." repeated here and there and sometimes underlined.

"The signage is helpful to me, too," the man continued. "The biggest mistake new people make coming out is having too much clutter on their signs. My current one just says, 'Cap and trade is C.I.A. bone.' Short but alluring, I think. My handouts fill out the argument. I find an economic message works best for Capitol Hill staffers. Better than a legal message. I leave those for my litigation." He narrowed his eyes. "Are you in politics?"

The Serial Stowaway shook her head.

"An attorney?"

"Well, I have some involvement in the law."

"Excellent," the man said. He closed the folder and, like a card sharp, shuffled the one below it to the top. He opened it, withdrew the stapled document, and handed it to The Serial Stowaway. "I'd love your thoughts about the argument here. It's a new legal angle for me."

The Serial Stowaway looked at the document but did not immediately take it.

"If you don't mind," the man said, sounding and looking embarrassed. "I don't want to be one of those overbearing men talking to a woman on an airplane. Or a novice writer asking a famous author to read his manuscript. This is just colleague to colleague. If you don't mind, of course."

"I don't mind," The Serial Stowaway said, and meant it because she would not have said it otherwise. Here is what she read.

Federal Court
District of Columbia

Death Penalty Action
[Execution scheduled January 26, 2022]

Peter Truett, *pro se*

154 13th Str. SE, No. 4
Washington D.C. 20003
(202) 320-3638
v.
Central Intelligence Agency [CIA]
Washington D.C. 20505
(703) 482-0623

Complaint
In re Walton Wilmot Moore

May it please the Court,

1. Walton Wilmot Moore is a death row convict, inmate number 127839, Osborn Correctional Institute,
Somers, Connecticut.
2. Peter Truett is a *pro se* litigant in Washington D.C.,
in other litigation alleging a series of ongoing assaults undertaken against him in Washington D.C. by agencies of
the United States government in what is ultimately a con-
spiratorial manner. A "42 U.S.C. 1986" allegation MUST
include a real conspiracy BUT not all participants in the
1986 activity have to be a party to it, and Truett has acted
against others in trying to expose it.

The Serial Stowaway flipped the sheet over and at the top
of the next saw, "Case 1:04-cv-36287-RWR Document 1
page 2 of 21." She continued reading.

3. Aspects of that conspiracy have very clearly been
planned and undertaken in Connecticut—most blatantly
the seizure of up to thirty-five thousand dollars [$35,000]
in Glastonbury, Connecticut [Attachment A, Re: Estate

and Trust u/a Heather S. Livesey—Second Partial Distribution dated October 15, 1993], but more important is the structure of communication and interaction [including survey, planning/grooming *which is truly pathetic*, scheduling, and consummating] made manifest in Connecticut. In some instances that has included CLEAR and BLATANT travel, equipment/material utilization, post-operation material handling and storage [very likely including indexing and file retrieval capabilities—winter images shown in the summertime.] *Unmistakable* and intended to be *unmistakable*. A FEW examples of *many* instances include in sequence by date:

A. [May 18 2010] Jasper Pine and Harold Anthony, thought to be residents of Connecticut and graduates of Naylor High School class of 1981 CLEARLY coordinated and controlled [staged] by someone totally apart from any remote family claim,

B. [June 19 2010] Andrew Godwin NOT a resident of Connecticut but traveling across state lines to participate in the conspiracy at 1812 Albritton Avenue in Glastonbury in *winter months* though not consummated or utilized until *June*,

C. [April 13 2011] Baird Archer, NOT a resident of Connecticut but traveling across state lines to participate in the conspiracy outside Town Pharmacy at a shopping center on the New London Turnpike in Glastonbury. EXPLICIT use by Archer of a medical diagnosis and advocacy hugely diminishing to Truett. Can't get around it—he is 'Baird the nuthouse supervisor' and he has been repeatedly made a party to the conspiracy for exactly that reason.

Connecticut involvement in assaults on Truett in Washington D.C. has progressed to the point of including Joseph I. Lieberman, at that time Senator from Connecticut, who Truett separately acts against in *Truett v. Lieberman* 03cv01463, though that case appears to have been stayed pending the outcome of a 372(c) filing. Former Senator Edward M. Kennedy, not of Connecticut but of border-sharing Massachusetts, also undertook acts against Truett.

The Serial Stowaway turned the page, and the man apparently named Peter Truett said, "This is what to me is the interesting part. Legally."

The Serial Stowaway continued reading.

4. *Moore* also involves huge distinct patterns of communication and interaction. That includes with and among various state agencies and media sources, undertaken by Moore himself and various others involved in *Moore* including attorneys, investigators, and doctors [citing specifically Marth J.H. Elliott, *The Connecticut Law Tribune,* April 29 1996 but elsewhere as well] and that has very definitely included medical opinions and advocacies.

5. The very nature of *Moore* made such opinions and advocacies unavoidable [high-profile sanity question]. To his surprise, however, in *Moore* Truett finds the calculated and orchestrated patterns of communication including medical opinions and advocacies *resemble those in his own matters*, which leads him to very much anticipate similar CIA or other agency involvement in *Moore. Grateful for the opportunity, Truett wants to use Moore as a pry bar to investigate CIA and other covert agency activity in Connecticut to date and ongoing.*

In other words: Truett's gotta guy gonna die in January and he wants to use him now.

The man apparently named Peter Truett said, "Well, it goes on, but you get the idea. It was dismissed, of course, but I devastated the court's opinion in my reply. Ancient history now, although I'm still working on getting increased scrutiny of CIA activities."

The Serial Stowaway handed back the paper. A flight attendant, not the one who had confronted the young man, approached with a cart. The man named Peter Truett gestured toward his crowded tray as an explanation for refusing a beverage and snack. The Serial Stowaway, thinking about the protein bars in her canvas bag, also declined. When the attendant and cart had made its way past their row and perhaps several others, the young man wearing the track suit appeared and, looking past the man named Peter Truett, said, "There you are," and asked for his backpack, which The Serial Stowaway passed to Peter Truett and he passed to the young man, who eyed it skeptically and walked back toward his seat. A few minutes later, the attendant who had participated in the contretemps appeared in the distance. Around the corner of the seat in front of her, The Serial Stowaway saw the flight attendant slow to glance at the young man in the track suit, the bag on his lap, and then slow as she approached the row containing The Serial Stowaway and the man named Peter Truett. Surreptitiousness apparently was not in this flight attendant's character, for she stared openly at Truett and The Serial Stowaway before proceeding another few rows and returning fore.

The Serial Stowaway glanced at Truett, who was looking at her with eyebrows raised.

She said, "CIA?"

He shrugged in a way that suggested he thought the probability lay in that direction, and they both were silent.

At her age, which at this time was sixty-four, The Serial Stowaway, like others her age, from time to time found that she required rest during the daytime. In her avocation, however, the need for daytime rest sometimes arose when alertness was necessary, specifically, on an airplane. The Serial Stowaway had therefore developed the necessary ability to sink into something approximating sleep while remaining attentive to the sounds around her. When those sounds were pleasant, well, so much the better.

"I am going to close my eyes," The Serial Stowaway said to Peter Truett, "but I am listening if you would like to tell me about meeting Senator Kennedy."

Truett nodded as though agreeing to a pact, waited until The Serial Stowaway's eyes had been closed for several seconds, and began, his mouth close enough to her ear for his words to be heard at low volume. Through her semi-slumber, she perceived Truett's telling of the following story.

Truett encountered Senator Edward Kennedy four times. He would, he said, refer to these as Kennedy One through Kennedy Four.

In the early morning hours of July 21, 2007, an image sequence featuring Edward Kennedy threatening "vascular dementia" accompanied by a distinct gesture and action sequence was induced in Truett's brain. The action in the image sequence centered around a full-size luxury black Ford or Mercury automobile as evidenced by the shape of the rear window on the driver's side.

Taking place in full daylight, that image sequence was likely recorded a day or two previous and included an image of another individual's body viewed briefly from the neck down (implying either Mr. Kennedy filmed the other person or two people were present besides Kennedy at time of filming).

The image sequence was accompanied by a recorded audio track featuring Mr. Kennedy saying "vascular dementia" in addition to the gesture.

"The most generous interpretation possible of the sequence following the threat," Truett told The Serial Stowaway, "was that Kennedy was offering me a job literally including a suit worn by a man 'viewed from the neck down' and a large black Ford or Mercury."

This sequence, Truett said, was "Kennedy One."

The next incident took place on September 18, 2008. Immediately after filing his appeal brief to Truett v United States, Truett was returning home via Constitution Avenue and witnessed an individual associated with Senator Kennedy conspicuously maneuvering around the same or a similar black full-sized Ford or Mercury double-parked on Constitution Avenue in front of the Russell Office Building in a manner designed to be seen by Truett as evidenced by a combination of gestures, expressions, and movements.

This sequence, Truett said, was "Kennedy Two."

Truett conceded that the next incident did not feature

Senator Kennedy in person, but nevertheless belonged among his Kennedy encounters, as would be seen. In the early morning hours of October 13, 2008, another image/audio sequence was induced in Truett's brain, this time featuring an actor intended to closely resemble Mr. Kennedy. This image sequence took place in and immediately outside of a saloon-type of bar with rough finishes. The image sequence was accompanied by an audio track featuring the actor saying "beer for eleven dollars" or words to that effect.

Upon identifying the actor as an actor and not Kennedy, who the actor resembled, Truett was punitively radiated sufficiently to lead him to believe the actor was intended to represent Kennedy.

This sequence, Truett said, was "Kennedy Three."

In the early morning hours of May 6, 2009, another image sequence featuring Mr. Kennedy was induced in Truett's brain. Taking place in the wintertime with a winter sun and outdoor setting viewed out a window, this image sequence featured Mr. Kennedy in the basement or ground-level first floor of a house, was obviously prerecorded (because it was a winter scene shown in May), and was accompanied by an audio track featuring Senator Kennedy saying, "I'd rent a tuxedo, and somebody'd buy me a drink" or words to that effect, to which Truett replied with an observation about "liability," following which Mr. Kennedy grunted or made some other audible response that was not a word.

This sequence, Truett said, was "Kennedy Four."

At this point, Truett excused himself to go to the restroom, and The Serial Stowaway remained in her state of semi-slumber.

Truett returned with news. He had used the first-class restroom—"Fuck these classist restroom rules."—and overheard the broad-shouldered, broad-haired specially-uniformed flight attendant using the word "stowaway" in an obviously private conversation with another attendant, a conversation that stopped the moment the higher ranking attendant perceived that Truett was within earshot.

The Serial Stowaway nodded. Truett appeared unruffled, just conveying information, and he did not pursue the matter. The Serial Stowaway's eyes still closed, her state of relaxation if anything deeper, said, "How do they put things into your brain. I mean, specifically, how is that done? I'm going to keep my eyes closed, but I'm listening."

Truett explained that while working in Japan from 1994 to 2000 on the New Unified Theater construction project, he was drugged and kidnapped from his apartment in Tokyo, and a system of neuroprosthetics was surreptitiously installed in his skull and brain by a person named Dorian Vick, who is affiliated with the CIA. The neuroprosthetic system is, based on Truett's research, composed of microscopic wires in the dura of the skull—that is, outside the brain-blood barrier—with additional electrodes on or near the hypothalamus, relatively deep in the brain. Additional prosthetics, probably uranium, thin film electrodes, and wire, were installed, also surreptitiously, elsewhere in Truett's body and skull.

"The system may be of Japanese manufacture," Truett said, "but the stronger likelihood is that it came from the

University of Michigan."

Truett explained that the neuroprosthetic system was developed by the United States related to verification of Soviet nuclear weapons, although the United States never made a security classification claim despite ample opportunity in previous litigation against the United States…here Truett paused to unearth and consult a document from his briefcase…including Truett v. United States 02-0279 RWR (D.C.), Appeal 02-7870, Petition for Writ of Certiorari (which he noted was denied) 02-7875, and Petition for Rehearing.

"But let me get back to the system itself," Truett said, seeming embarrassed by his digression. The neuroprosthetic system, he explained, provides remote human operators the capability to expose Truett's head, skull, and brain to highly focused electromagnetic radiation on an ongoing basis, often inducing sensation. "And often extreme pain," Truett said, not seeking sympathy, just clarifying. The system provides the operator with the capability to monitor and stimulate neural impulse effectively equating to monitoring Truett's thoughts, vision, speech, and under certain conditions— "Here," Truett said, "is where Kennedy One through Four come in," inducing image and audio sequences in his brain.

"As for the CIA role," Truett said, with the tone of one concluding, as a flight attendant announced final walk-through prior to landing, "I'll just summarize by saying that various groups, including the CIA, and individuals radiate and monitor me, and they have access to data resulting from radiating and monitoring me, and they develop and coordinate plans to radiate me and to keep me under physical surveillance—by people on the street or in buildings or on modes of transportation like buses and airplanes, which is often coordinated with the surveillance by electromagnetic radiation. I assume that the electromagnetic-radiation-enabled monitoring can take place while I am in flight."

Having been reminded by a passing attendant that he needed to close his tray, Truett began collecting his documents, pausing only long enough to show The Serial Stowaway an illustration he had drawn of the neuroprosthetic installation in his brain from page 21 (of 44) of case 1:03-cv-01599-RWR, Plaintiff's Response to Strickland Notification in Three Parts plus Affidavits (Opposition to Defendant's Motion to Dismiss) and to say that the reason most often given for dismissing his lawsuits was "lack of subject matter expertise," at which he gave a laugh similar to the jolly fatman's belly-laugh of British-born actor Sydney Greenstreet, who began his acting career at age 61, the same age at which The Serial Stowaway began her career.

The plane landed, as all planes must. The passengers crowded into the aisle to depart, as all passengers must. Truett, from his aisle seat, stood and motioned The Serial Stowaway to precede him, but after they stood a moment, he leaned over, said, "Not that you need protecting, but I would consider this an honor, colleague to colleague," and edged past her. There they stood as preparations were being made at the front of the cabin for their departure.

The line, as all lines do, eventually began to move. To The Serial Stowaway's practiced perception, the progress was slower than most lines of airplane egress.

The passenger immediately ahead of Truett in the creeping line was a woman whose shoulders, one at a time, with each step, moved up and down like a steering wheel on a winding road. The person ahead of this person was the tracksuited young man, plump backpack draped over one shoulder. A few steps further, when the woman's right shoulder dipped, Truett stretched his long arm forward, extended his fingers stiffly, and poked the young man's backpack.

The young man looked behind him, looked around him, and pulled the backpack strap higher on his shoulder.

After another step, Truett poked the backpack again. The young man looked behind him, saw that the woman to his rear was looking away, eyed Truett, and saw that Truett, who had removed his glasses and placed them in his breast pocket, was staring at him not aggressively, but directly and steadily.

Mumbling what may have been the word "whatever," the young man commenced to look alternately forward and backward, his face showing the belligerence of one convinced he can handle any situation, except, perhaps, one that he could not understand.

When Truett poked the backpack once more, the young man's head flipped around to glare. He opened his mouth to speak, but Truett beat him, saying, "That's a nice backpack, buddy," in a voice loud yet friendly and pointed enough to freeze the young man's planned response. As the young man tried to determine whether he should say thank you and, if so, whether he could say that in a tone that communicated both annoyance and command, Truett continued. "Big, too.

Whatchya got in there, buddy?"

By this time, the line was moving at a slightly quicker pace, and the woman between Truett and the young man had stepped aside.

Truett went on, louder, but still friendly. "Looks just the right size for a human head. You have a human head in there?"

The young man turned fully around, walking backward as the line proceeded.

"A really big head," Truett declared. "I'm thinking the head of a president."

The line at this point was well into the first-class section, and the broad-haired, broad-shoulder, specially uniformed attendant was visible even to The Serial Stowaway, who at her height could look only around and not over the people ahead of her. With the attendant was a white-shirted, gold-braid capped, uniformed male, surely a pilot, as well as a male in the very-dark-navy-blue uniform of law enforcement.

Truett, friendly, very loud, and Socratic, said, "You know which president had the largest head?" He turned to take in others in the vicinity. "Anyone? Largest head? He wasn't the tallest, but close...anyone? It's Bill Clinton." This last was a joyous proclamation.

By now, the young man with the backpack, the man named Peter Truett, and The Serial Stowaway were but one or two people away from the three authority figures arrayed between the cockpit and the exit.

"Wow," Truett said in the tone of a stage actor projecting surprise to a large audience, "you got BILL CLINTON's head in there?" Without waiting for a reply—what, after all, could the young man say except "no," which anyone in the surrounding area would stipulate—Truett directed himself toward the attendant, pilot, and law enforcement official, proclaiming with a mixture of alarm and revelation, his volume soaring, "Hey, hey, you better stop this guy. He has Bill Clinton's head in his backpack. I mean it." He raised his voice even more. "The ACTUAL head of William Jefferson CLINTON is in THAT VERY BACKPACK!"

As the three officials, with the calm of those experienced in approaching the creatively unruly, surrounded Truett, The Serial Stowaway slid around the tableau.

At an adjacent gate area, The Serial Stowaway sat, withdrew one of the young man's protein bars, and attempted to eat it, although she found it quite difficult to bite off and chew, and found the flavor to be not really any flavor at all. However, food was a necessity, and she finished one of the bars, returning the other to her canvas tote for later.

The bar having stuck here and there in The Serial Stowaway's teeth and left pieces in her throat, she found the nearest restroom and drank from the adjacent water fountain. Raising her head, she faced Truett.

"You seem surprised to see me," he said.

She nodded.

He continued, "Oh, I emerged unscathed and unrestrained. Once you passed, I became as docile as a doormat and as reasonable as a referee. I told them that I was a history buff and that I had read somewhere that Bill Clinton had the largest head of any U.S. president and that I was just joshing with the guy in the track suit, whom I assured them I had known at good ol' Allegheny State College. They didn't believe me, but they let me go."

The Serial Stowaway nodded.

Truett asked, "What are your plans?"

The Serial Stowaway looked around the concourse. "Oh, I'll be walking around a bit. Then I need to head back to Chicago."

It was Truett's turn to nod. Resuming his Sydney Greenstreet voice, this time the throaty, confidential variety, Truett said, "Well, then, madam, I suppose we must say good-bye. Unless…" The skin around Truett's eyes, still uncovered by spectacles, crinkled. "Unless you care to undertake the Constantinople expedition with us. You don't? Well, madam, frankly I'd like to have you along. You're a person to my liking, a person of many resources and nice judgment." He shrugged, and puffed out his cheeks as Greenstreet did in *The Maltese Falcon*. "Well, madam, the shortest farewells are the best. Adieu."

He tipped his straw hat and then bowed, holding his hand as though around a rotund midsection. He replaced his eyeglasses and started off, first in Greenstreet's relaxed and magisterial stride, then, leaning slightly forward, with unmistakable purpose.

Chapter 6:
The Serial Stowaway
and the Superstitious Mother

Thirty-eight miles northwest of Cook County Department of Corrections, where The Serial Stowaway would later spend one hundred and forty-four days, twenty-five miles north of Chicago's O'Hare Airport, three miles from a farm-like facility that segregates people with developmental disabilities from others in the population in what the facility calls a "family of peers," and nine-tenths of a mile west of the Libertyville, Illinois, Village Hall, was a blocky, yellow-brick three-story building containing what the owners called "senior residences." Up the building's crawling elevator (stairs existed but were rarely used) to the top floor, in a front-facing apartment at the building's center, in the apartment's sole bedroom, where The Serial Stowaway slept when not in transit, on the tiny closet's highest shelf, was a white box.

The box was the type with a slip-on lid, the type used in the law office where The Serial Stowaway had worked for folders too dated to be of immediate use but too recent to go into deep storage. After her mother's death, from among her possessions, The Serial Stowaway had selected this box to keep.

Although the box was not sealed, The Serial Stowaway had never lifted the lid, not even before choosing to keep it. She had chosen this box for two reasons. First, because it was so pristine, as though The Serial Stowaway's mother had purchased and packed the box shortly before her death. Second, because on the lid was written, in thin, black marker with a hand firm in its conviction, the notation "9:44."

The Serial Stowaway's mother believed that forty-four minutes after the hour of nine, both a.m. and p.m., had special importance, although The Serial Stowaway had never been able to determine the precise nature of that importance. From the time her household purchased its first digital clock sometime in The Serial Stowaway's early teens, The Serial Stowaway recalled that her mother on most days, sometimes in the morning, sometimes in the evening, frequently both, would point at the clock and say "There it is again. Every time I look at a clock, any clock, it says nine forty-four."

This she said sometimes with the delight of adding one more piece to the overwhelming pile of evidence proving her thesis, sometimes with the smugness of disproving anyone narrow enough in their thinking to doubt her thesis, and sometimes, especially later in her life, with the determination of one staying on a path chosen long ago that at one time seemed heading toward triumph but that now appeared it could just as easily lead to infamy.

The Serial Stowaway's mother used the same variations

in tone when pointing through her windshield in the evening to extinguished streetlights, these being evidence to support another thesis she held, which was that her approach caused streetlights to extinguish.

At no point in her formal education did The Serial Stowaway encounter the concepts of the self-fulfilling prophesy or confirmation bias, but she had no problem developing the ideas all by herself, recognizing that the things her mother chose to notice were random and that her mother's notice of them escalated the more she noticed them.

To The Serial Stowaway, growing up, what raised her mother's fixations from mere idiosyncrasy to something weightier was her mother's belief that she had some control over the appearance of nine forty-four and the extinguishment of streetlights. This confidence gave her mother, in The Serial Stowaway's eyes, a grand presence, like having a mother who was a combination of queen and magician.

After choosing the white box labeled "9:44" to keep from among her mother's possessions, The Serial Stowaway had not felt any compulsion either to avoid or investigate its contents. The box was simply there, perhaps as a reminder of her mother, perhaps just as something to have on the closet shelf, The Serial Stowaway having few possessions herself.

One spring afternoon, a year after her mother's death, a year after moving into this apartment, a year after she had begun her ritual train rides, The Serial Stowaway happened to look at her kitchen clock, which read one thirty-seven, and realized that since her mother's death she had not noticed nine forty-four on the face of any digital timepiece, nor had any streetlights gone dark when she approached. Having this realization, The Serial Stowaway did not feel any particular way. She did not miss her mother or her mother's quirks. She did not desire to understand her mother any better than she already did. Having this realization served only to remind her of the box labeled "9:44," and to further cause her to think that because she was not riding trains that day she needed to do something else, and to further cause her to think that she might use this time to look inside her mother's white file box, particularly because, now that she remembered the box, she also remembered how, when she used such boxes at the law office, their lids were so easy and pleasant to slip off and on, in contrast to the awkwardness of opening other types of cartons.

These thoughts having converged, The Serial Stowaway stood on her tiptoes and extended her fingertips to nudge and then pull the box from the closet's high shelf.

Placing the box on her bed, she felt no need for ceremonial taking of a beat or inhaling and exhaling. She simply removed the lid bearing "9:44," placed it beside the box on the bed, and, seeing a loosely packed collection of items, stuck in her hand.

One by one, she removed the items and placed them on her bed. Each appeared new. Each was in original packaging, if packaging were called for, and had original tags affixed by adhesive or plastic string. When she had finished removing all but the last item, she had these arrayed on her thin, olive-green bedspread:

A slatted wooden spoon

A pink vegetable scrubber

A bottle of white liquid correction fluid

A packet of twenty thank-you note cards

A group of four D-size batteries

A four-tool, nine-function, red Swiss Army knife

A medium-blue, medium-bristle toothbrush

A ball of gold yarn

A white washcloth

A baseball

A turkey baster

A pair of gray work gloves

A plastic bottle of sixty ashwagandha capsules

An acrylic French nail kit, white, medium length

A royal-blue air horn mounted on a yellow canister

A fifty-foot bundle of white, cotton, braided, three-sixteenth-inch clothesline

The last item that The Serial Stowaway withdrew from the box she examined more closely than the others because it was so different from the others. The other items from the box were disparate from one another in almost every imaginable way except that they were new. This item was old. Because the item was a book, had The Serial Stowaway consulted the copyright page she would have seen how old it was, the book having been published in 1964. The book was hardcover with yellowing deckle-edged paper and a dust jacket chipped here and there on its corners. The dust jacket's color was that of newsprint, and on it was a photo-collage consisting of five items:

Two torn pieces of paper featuring radical and radically dissimilar fonts; together, these pieces gave the title of the book, which was *A Taste of Campari*.

One image, seemingly torn from a magazine, of a commercial airline in flight.

A portion of a road atlas showing the city of Seville and outlying areas.

A strip of crumpled white paper on which was typed by a manual typewriter: "by Keith Carlton."

The back cover had a black-and-white studio photograph of Mr. Carlton in dark suit and tie and white shirt, half-smiling, looking left of the camera, perhaps thinking about Seville.

Her bedspread now crowded with box, lid, and contents, The Serial Stowaway set the book on her pillow.

With only passing thought, The Serial Stowaway understood that any attempt to connect these items with nine forty-four would be futile. Her mother's mind was too idiosyncratic for such logical associations. Probably, no, certainly, the items did pertain to nine forty-four; her mother's mind was not incoherent, just idiosyncratic. As elusive as that connection might be, another connection was obvious: except for the book, the items were not only new but, based on the unopened packaging, unexamined. Thus, the items were acquired not for use but for some other reason. One possible reason, The Serial Stowaway thought, would be solely to have the items, as a collector collects. And as a collector collects items within a certain theme, this line of thought led back to these items having some connection to nine forty-four. The

Serial Stowaway picked up an item and then another and then another, looking at their labels, their prices, their product numbers. As might be expected, she saw the occasional nine and four and even once two fours in sequence, but nothing to suggest a connection with nine forty-four any stronger than a frayed thread.

Another possible reason for The Serial Stowaway's mother to have these items—for anyone to have any items—was pleasure in the act of acquiring them. The Serial Stowaway's mother had not in her life shown any special interest in the act of shopping. Well, if not shopping, thought The Serial Stowaway, perhaps shoplifting.

As quickly as the thought emerged, The Serial Stowaway could see the idea in action: her mother dropping items into her canvas shoulder bag, not exactly heedless of the potential consequences, but appearing heedless. The Serial Stowaway pictured her mother's shoplifting as an evolving career, starting with smaller risks and larger apprehension and working toward larger risks and smaller apprehension.

And then there was the book. The Serial Stowaway lifted it from her pillow. She had rarely seen her mother read a book. The condition of the book's cover and spine suggested it had been read, perhaps many times, but of course, it may have been read by someone other than The Serial Stowaway's mother. And its being old did not mean it had not been stolen; perhaps The Serial Stowaway's mother had snitched it from a Goodwill shop. She returned the book to her pillow.

The Serial Stowaway replaced the items from her bedspread into the box, handling them with no particular care.

Before tossing the book into the box to join the other items, The Serial Stowaway thumb-flipped the pages from back to front. They threw off the pleasant smell of basement. About a third of the way through, a dark line flew past her vision. She backtracked, turning pages slowly, and there, on page 58, underlined in what looked like the same black ink that marked the lid of this box, was the following sentence: "Sliding three twenty-dollar bills authoritatively across the counter, Delmont requested that the demure clerk give him a one-way ticket on the 9:44 flight to Seville."

The Serial Stowaway smiled and shut the book. But instead of tossing it back into the box, she placed it on her nightstand.

That night, The Serial Stowaway sat up in bed holding the book open to the page spread containing the underlined sentence. She read the sentence several times. Then she read the sentence within a few sentences that occurred before and after it. Then she read that group of sentences again. Then again. In all, she read the passage thirteen times. This is the passage The Serial Stowaway read:

> Seville, Delmont thought. Not a bad spot to stalk one's prey.
>
> Quickly transferring a few sports shirts, slacks, undershorts and handkerchiefs from dresser drawers to overnight bag—which always contained a ready-to-go toiletries case, Delmont hopped a cab on the corner of 83rd and Third. He enjoyed the twinkling lights against the deepening slate color of the sky as the cab, with a minimum of conversation from the driver, darted competently toward Idlewild Airport.

In the terminal, Delmont chose the ticket counter staffed by the prettiest attendant. Appreciatively eying her shy, moon-shaped face and what elements of her shape the waist-high counter and sexless uniform allowed to be discerned, Delmont slid three twenty-dollar bills authoritatively across the counter and requested that the demure clerk give him a one-way ticket on the 9:44 flight to Seville.

Breezing from ticket counter to terminal bar, for a quick scotch and soda on the rocks, to gate B twenty-three, Delmont was waved onto the plane by an attendant more statuesque and better at eye contact than the woman who had sold him his ticket. He settled into his assigned seat, sighed happily, and readied himself for a peaceful sleep on the overnight flight, knowing when he awoke it would be to the sunshine of Seville, and to whatever path toward the truth his wits could uncover.

After her multiple readings of this passage, The Serial Stowaway set the book back on her nightstand, closed her eyes, and embarked on a journey.

In this stage of her journey, in the state between consciousness and sleep, images and thoughts and sensations gently jostled within The Serial Stowaway: the cover of the book, Demont's manner of travel, her mother's box of perhaps-shoplifted treasures, her mother's concern for nine forty-four and extinguishing streetlights, her own ritual of train travel.

In some ways, this state of The Serial Stowaway resembled that described by William Wordsworth in "Lines Composed a Few Miles above Tintern Abbey, On Revisiting the Banks of the Wye during a Tour. July 13, 1798":

Until the breath of this corporeal frame
And even the motion of our human blood
Almost suspended, we are laid asleep
In body, and become a living soul:
While with an eye made quiet by the power
Of harmony, and the deep power of joy,
We see into the life of things.

In another way, this act of seeing "into the life of things," so quiet and harmonious for Wordsworth, also resembled the more animated multi-step process of creative insight described by mathematician, theoretical physicist, and philosopher of science Henri Poincaré.

Poincaré is known for, among many accomplishments, creating one of the founding documents in chaos theory (which, alas, or perhaps appropriately, contained a mathematical error when first issued), showing that the stability of such systems as the solar system cannot be demonstrated. In his 1908 essay "Le Raisonnement Mathématique," Poincaré told the story of writing his first examination of Fuchsian functions. For more than two weeks, Poincaré struggled to accomplish his goal of showing there could not be any functions such as those he ultimately called Fuchsian functions, doing so through hour after hour of examining various combinations, with no results. "I was then," he wrote, "very ignorant."

He continued, "One evening, contrary to my custom, I drank black coffee and could not sleep. Ideas rose in crowds; I felt them collide until pairs interlocked, so to speak, making a stable combination. By the next morning I had established the existence of a class of Fuchsian functions." From there, with conscious deliberation and without difficulty, Poincaré applied this insight in forming "the series I have called theta-Fuchsian."

All that is interesting, instructive, and relevant, but the next step in Poincaré's journey of ideas is perhaps more so in illuminating the journey of The Serial Stowaway. Poincaré left the city where he was living to make a geological excursion.

> The changes of travel made me forget my mathematical work. Having reached Coutances, we entered an omnibus to go some place or other. At the moment when I put my foot on the step the idea came to me, without anything in my former thoughts seeming to have paved the way for it, that the transformations I had used to define the Fuchsian functions were identical with those of non-Euclidean geometry. I did not verify the idea; I should not have had time, as, upon taking my seat in the omnibus, I went on with a conversation already commenced, but I felt a perfect certainty. On my return to Caen, for conscience's sake I verified the result at my leisure.

A far better-known version of Poincaré's journey from quest to not knowing to knowing is the story of Mary Shelley's creation of the novel *Frankenstein*. The critical portion of Shelley's story occurs after the best-known part: Shelley and her friends giving themselves an assignment to write a scary story, Shelley going to bed on a stormy night, and Shelley dreaming the Frankenstein idea and narrative. The critical part of Shelley's journey of ideas occurs after the dream. Shelley gives her account of this moment in her own introduction to the book's 1831 edition. Having woken from her dream, Shelley recalled, "I wished to exchange the ghastly image of my fancy for the realities around." However, she went on:

> I could not so easily get rid of my hideous phantom; still it haunted me. I must try to think of something else. I recurred to my ghost story,—my tiresome unlucky ghost story! O! if I could only contrive one which would frighten my reader as I myself had been frightened that night!
>
> Swift as light and as cheering was the idea that broke in upon me. "I have found it! What terrified me will terrify others; and I need only describe the spectre which had haunted my midnight pillow." On the morrow I announced that I had thought of a story.

Here, Shelley puts a brighter light on the moment Poincaré describes of his seemingly unbidden insight when stepping onto the omnibus. As with Poincaré, the assignment and the fulfillment of that assignment were both within Mary Shelley, they were within sight of one another, but they were segregated from one another: "O! if I could only contrive one which would frighten my reader as I myself had been frightened that night!" They were segregated. And then, the previous steps in the journey of alternating consciousness and semiconsciousness coalescing, they were together, and an idea, a wholly new idea, was formed.

As profound as this coalescence was, it was not the journey's terminal but another junction. What, then, comes after that moment of discovery that "I had thought of a story" or the principle of Fuchsian functions? According to Amy Lowell in her essay "The Process of Making Poetry," what comes after is this: "Suddenly words are there, and there with an imperious insistence which brooks no delay. They must be written down immediately or an acute suffering comes on, a distress almost physical, which is not relieved until the poem is given right of way."

To these examples testified to by Henri Poincaré and Mary Shelley of crossing the mental divide between the moment of not having an idea and then having an idea, and by Amy Lowell of the subsequent compulsion to act, it is possible to add the experience upon waking that morning of The Serial Stowaway—and its sequel.

The Serial Stowaway's journey took her through three ideas en route to one ultimate idea. These ideas could, perhaps, be called simple, but such judgment is a convenience of distance. All ideas are profound to those who have them, and to suggest otherwise is to deny the joy of life.

The Serial Stowaway's first idea was how smoothly the man in this passage of the book, this person called Delmont, passed the ticket counter and on into the terminal, and from the terminal onto the airplane. Effortless—better still, delightful! The Serial Stowaway's air travel experience was limited to one flight to Orlando, Florida, with a high school group in 1979, but like every even moderately sentient being, The Serial Stowaway understood that the modern air-travel process, for all but the very wealthy, was complex. One had to make reservations ahead of time. One needed proof of such reservations and officially issued, photograph-bearing identification. One needed to pass through security screening so scrupulous that even the innocent frequently found themselves being physically frisked and their belongings poked and squeezed, unpacked and scrutinized.

Which made Delmont's breezy exchange of cash for a ticket and a glidepath to a seat as intoxicating as it was anachronistic.

The second idea was that, were Delmont to be viewed as within the elongated dumbbell of The Serial Stowaway's mental picture of her train travels, the dumbbells being the termini and the handles the route, his friction-free movement from ticket counter to terminal to airplane accomplished something that didn't seem quite possible: Delmont had, with no particular effort, broken through the rounded end of the dumbbell that had always served not as a conduit but an impermeable terminal for The Serial Stowaway's travels. That Delmont could so easily burst through such a barrier—well, that was quite an idea.

The third and penultimate idea was that the formerly impermeable terminus of the airport ticketing area could, once penetrated, take one onto another path, in this case, Demont's overnight flight, another elongated dumbbell handle, another time and place between a new origin and a new destination, another vibrating container, and one that a person could enjoy for twice as long, three times as long, four times as long—more!—as The Serial Stowaway's periods on the Metra between Libertyville and Chicago.

Delmont sure was a fortunate guy.

The Serial Stowaway's fourth and final idea—like those of Shelley and Poincaré—came only after a pause.

The Serial Stowaway's usual waking time was 5:30 a.m., after which she began the methodical performance of her morning routine. This morning's routine, however, was different in one way: Accompanying The Serial Stowaway on these activities was the summary of her third idea from the night before: that Delmont sure was a fortunate guy. The thought was a conscious one; The Serial Stowaway may even have said those words aloud between sips of tea or between rinsing her hair and soaping her body.

That morning, a spoonful of grocery-store-brand corn flakes on its way to her mouth, The Serial Stowaway had another idea. This was her fourth idea, and a most critical one in her journey. That idea was this: "Why should the opportunity to permeate, to so smoothly, so joyously permeate, the barrier to air travel be the sole domain of Delmont in the 1964 novel (she had by now checked its publication date) *A Taste of Campari*? Why shouldn't I, thought The Serial Stowaway, do that also, and just as effortlessly?"

As described by Amy Lowell, insights such as this one by The Serial Stowaway are launching points for a great deal of work. Mathematicians need to work out their formulas. Physicists need to work out their equations. Sculptors need to shape their material. Writers need to put words on paper.

As difficult as this stage of actualization may be for any individual, one may argue that it was less challenging for Henri Poincaré or Mary Shelley, who were working with familiar tools even if in unfamiliar ways, than for The Serial Stowaway, who had neither experience in, nor any concrete notion of how one might go about, moving through the airport ticketing area to the inside of an airplane in an effortless fashion. The Serial Stowaway had only the idea that if a character in her mother's book could do it, and if The Serial Stowaway desired to do it, then she could, and she would, do it too.

The next morning, The Serial Stowaway's ideas having "an imperious insistence which brooks no delay," and needing to be put into action "immediately or an acute suffering comes on," The Serial Stowaway stood across the corridor from the entrance to security checkpoint four, indicated in Chicago's O'Hare Airport by a startlingly saturated yellow sign high in the air, seemingly poised to crash onto those below at any moment. The time was nine forty-four.

Chapter 7:
The Serial Stowaway
and the Reality TV Star

At this point in The Serial Stowaway's career, it was inevitable that she should have received some attention in the popular media. Arrests in Chicago, San Francisco, and Washington, D.C. (when she attempted to board a flight after her adventure with the professional protester) were of sufficient number to establish a pattern discernible to a handful of intrepid reporters, and after that it was a simple matter for the reporters that followed to add accounts of each subsequent arrest to that base story, thus through sheer repetition hammering into some subset of the public consciousness a recognizable individual. She was even given a nickname: The Serial Stowaway.

Thus, we should not be surprised that The Serial Stowaway's adventures should eventually lead her to the Bright Lights of Show Business, and that this encounter would take place on a morning flight from The City That Never Sleeps, New York, New York, to The Entertainment Capital of the

World, Los Angeles, California.

At New York's LaGuardia Airport, to which she had flown from the Cleveland Hopkins International Airport and not exited past the TSA, The Serial Stowaway made it past the gate checkpoint by taking advantage of the distraction caused by an obviously inebriated woman who, having been denied access to the flight, was swinging her cell phone at the two gate agents as if it were a sword.

After two attempts to sit, both of which were thwarted by the arrival of a passenger with an assignment to that seat, The Serial Stowaway found herself a place between two fully credentialed members of the showbiz world—a discovery that occurred when the person on her right in the aisle seat, a stately woman with silver, side-swept hair, began to huff and puff theatrically over a document she was studying, and the person on The Serial Stowaway's left in the window seat, a man with a gigantic jaw mirrored by a gigantic black bouffant, sounding grateful for an excuse to begin a conversation, spoke across The Serial Stowaway to the stately woman in a what may have been a mock British accent at a volume louder than necessary to overcome the aircraft's ambient noise, "My dear, what horrible happening is ruining your morning?"

The stately woman's stateliness tottered as her voice teetered. "This," she said, pointing toward the document. "This *shit*. This shit *again*. It never *ends*."

"Do tell," the man said, hurrying to add, "I never tell."

After a brief back and forth and nudging of possibly feigned recollection, it turned out that the woman knew of the man, whose name was Francis November, formerly a publicist to A-list celebrities at the world-famous Artastic Agency, currently combining paid celebrity commentary on television with a budding life-coaching business based on insights gleaned from the stars, captured in his recently released book (which Mr. November almost embarrassedly produced from his seatback pocket and flashed) titled *Love Yourself and Other Life Lessons of the Glitterati*.

With no back and forth or need for feigned or otherwise unearthed recollection, the man had recognized this woman—celebrity, after all, being his passion and profession (truly a profession, for unlike so many content creators, he got paid)—as Clarissa Clarke, one half, most would say the lesser half, of the long-defunct comedy duo Lewis and Clarke, the Lewis half having gone on to movie stardom in roles both comic (initially) and dramatic (more recently), while Ms. Clarke had, well, been doing something; even Francis November was not sure what.

The recognitions recognized, the two shook hands across The Serial Stowaway, and Ms. Clarke resumed poking at the papers, now considerably worse for wear, in her hand, saying, "In my own bio, for chrissake. I did *not* approve this. But what can I expect from *reality* television? God."

The side-swept woman, resuming some of her stateliness, passed the document across The Serial Stowaway, managing to keep her finger on the offending passage enough for the bouffanted man to locate it, although he did not have to read it, because the not-quite-stately woman was reciting it in a tone simultaneously angry and melodic: "Clarissa first came to national attention as the straight person in the brilliant comedy duo of Lewis and Clarke."

"Ouch," Mr. November said, his British accent making the word a multisyllabic expression of fellow-feeling.

"Right?" Ms. Clarke said, with the sound of a pencil being snapped in half. "Why don't they just come right out and say I was the boring one holding back the brilliant Ms. Lewis? That's what they used to say before they stopped saying anything at all about me. Linda fucking Bauerlein said the same thing in *The New York Times* about that one pathetic movie we did." Clarissa recited with a similar mixture of singsong and anger, "'Ms. Clarke, for her pretty presence, rates a nod.' A *nod*! And as for my partner? 'Give Ms. Lewis enough time and the encouragement to go her own sweet way and she could turn out to be a great comedienne one of these happy days.'"

"Ouch to the second power," Mr. November said.

Still reciting: "'The way Ms. Lewis wears her beret, waves a cigarette holder in the air and addresses her party companions is mimicry at its best, rich with pathos.' And you know what? *I* was the one who told her she looked good in a beret!"

"Tragic," Mr. November said.

Still reciting: "'It is notable that Ms. Lewis' best moments are played by her alone. She is slowly taking over the act from Ms. Clarke. Just give her a couple of more years.'"

"You have quite a memory," Mr. November said.

Ms. Clarke's voice dropped in volume and increased in threat level: "Some things you don't forget."

Handing back the papers across The Serial Stowaway and ignoring a flight attendant's inquiry about beverage and snack desires, Mr. November asked, managing not to implicate career invisibility, what Ms. Clarke was up to these days. (Actually, he asked what "we" were up to these days, but he meant "you," and Ms. Clarke took it as such.)

Also ignoring the flight attendant (to whom The Serial Stowaway merely shrugged in resignation), Ms. Clarke flipped to the first page and poked it every few seconds as she explained the situation.

Clarissa Clarke had agreed to join, for one season, the cast of a reality television program called *D-Listed*—Mr. November nodded with a combination of recognition and condolence—in which several showbiz people who had tumbled off the cliff of celebrity but not quite hit the ground of oblivion are forced to live together in a house and, using intel provided by the producers, encouraged to remind one another of a) what might have been, b) those who had done them wrong, and c) actual shortcomings of talent, personality, looks, and character that may have contributed to their impending nonexistence.

Ms. Clarke flagged down a flight attendant and, over Bloody Marys (Ms. Clarke) and club sodas (Mr. November), and as the flight continued, Ms. Clarke regaled Mr. November with tales of slights and lost opportunities.

As Ms. Clarke told her tales, Mr. November deftly shifted her woes from self-pity to self-help with lessons learned from celebrities:

"Pause and step outside" (Lady Gaga).

"Allow yourself to be happy in the present moment" (George Clooney).

"Show interest in others so they will show interest in you" (Jennifer Lopez).

"Get a side hustle" (Edward Norton).

"Be honest with yourself about what your gut is telling you and trust it" (Bette Davis).

"Set an appointment with yourself once each quarter for personal reflection" (Brad Pitt).

"Avoid eating meat and dance often" (Bill Gates).

"Stay curious" (Faye Dunaway).

"Focus on gratitude" (Madonna).

"Avoid buying the cheapest product...or the most expensive one" (Tom Cruise).

"Eat almonds" (Christopher Walken).

"Include an 'interests' section in your resume" (Beyoncé).

"Be clear about what you will do and won't do" (Kim Kardashian).

"Accept that things will happen" (Jack Nicholson).

Ms. Clarke deftly eluded each of these placations, finally playing what she obviously considered her trump card of injustice dealt her by a malevolent universe, with voice shaking from the nearness of tears. "Even when she talked about the Lewis and Clarke breakup, she stole from me. She would say our breakup reminded her of this story: One person says to another person, 'Those are beautiful shoes you're wearing,' and the other person replies, 'Yes, but I'm the only one who knows how much they hurt.' God, have you ever heard such tripe? And everyone would just *gush* over how *sensitive* and *profound* that was, the *tears of a clown*, and all that. But I'll have you know it was *me* who was always telling *her* about how much my shoes hurt!'"

With that card played and Mr. November momentarily bereft of relevant celebrity wisdom, Ms. Clarke left her seat, presumably in search of a restroom, abandoning her papers—invitation letter, itinerary, biography—on her seat.

Quiet restored, Mr. November produced a handful of notecards, which he studied with bouffant tilted forward, occasionally closing his eyes.

During one of the closed-eyes moments, The Serial Stowaway plucked Ms. Clarke's papers from the seat and placed them in her canvas tote.

When the flight landed and the row containing The Serial Stowaway, Ms. Clarke, and Mr. November had been released from the walkway into the concourse and Ms. Clarke pinned Mr. November to a wall, asking him when they could get together for lunch and whether he was taking on clients ("for personal representation," she clarified, "not life coaching"), The Serial Stowaway accelerated past and toward the point at which friends, family, and fans were allowed to greet incoming passengers. There, The Serial Stowaway saw a dark-suited man holding an iPad screen displaying in large capital letters, "CLARISSA CLARKE." The Serial Stowaway approached and said, "I'm Ms. Clarke."

When the man asked about luggage, The Serial Stowaway shook her head. She followed the man through the terminal until, between shops labeled Chanel and Magic Johnson Sports, she saw one labeled Hollywood Style. After tugged the driver's sleeve and holding up a finger indicating that he should wait, she entered the store, stole a wide-brimmed camel-colored hat and pair of plastic cat's-eye sunglasses, and wearing both, tugged the driver's sleeve once more and pointed forward.

In the driver's pearl-gray Chrysler Pacifica, The Serial Stowaway withdrew the papers from her tote, lifted her sunglasses, and saw that she would be spending the next two nights at the D'accord Resort and Spa in El Segundo. The driver said, "D'accord?" and The Serial Stowaway looked up to see him looking at her in the rearview mirror.

"D'accord," she agreed, and settled back to watch, through her green-tinted lenses, the sun-soaked scenery, this being the first time she had departed an airport terminal— other than O'Hare on her way home to Libertyville—since her Hawaiian experience, glad that this time she was being driven in this comfortable vehicle rather than in a police car.

The driver pulled to the curb in front of what presumably was the central structure of the expansive property. He exited smartly with the intention of opening his passenger's door, but when he reached the right side saw that his passenger had already slid open her door and was in the process of dismounting. He started toward the rear compartment, recalled this passenger had no luggage, and watched her back as it moved toward the entrance. He tilted back his cap and scratched his head. These showbiz types, he thought. Either they want to be pampered, or they want to be left alone. No tip, he noted, glad that the agency that hired him had built fifteen percent into the fee.

Inside, The Serial Stowaway confronted a smattering of

registration kiosks being fed by a line, the placement of which required that people otherwise occupied in the lobby constantly cut through those in line. Soon enough, The Serial Stowaway saw herself being waved to by a figure whose distance-caused faintness was made more so by The Serial Stowaway's indoor sunglasses.

At the kiosk, The Serial Stowaway was met by a woman with a tastefully small rectangular gold nameplate that read "Melinda-Joy" pinned to the lapel of her slightly-too-large polyester suit jacket. Melinda-Joy, who had just been promoted to Assistant Front Desk Manager after toiling as Front Desk Agent for a much longer duration than others with far less command of the nuances of her position, demonstrated, if privately, that command by noticing at once that the woman before her, adjusting her broad-brimmed hat slightly to the left and nudging her sunglasses up the bridge of her nose, had never in her life worn such a hat nor indoor sunglasses.

Greeting this woman, Melinda-Joy said, "Good day, madam."

The day before, at 11:30 a.m., Melinda-Joy had been overheard saying "Good day" to a guest, and Melinda-Joy's supervisor, a man who wore a red silk dress scarf useful only to demonstrate his moderately higher salary, corrected her, noting that the time was not yet noon and so the proper greeting was "Good morning." To this correction, he added his favorite admonition, "Words matter," paused, and continued, "especially in your new position, Melinda-Joy." Hearing this, Melinda-Joy, who had won a district spelling bee championship in middle school, won a state speech champion in high school, and currently wrote a popular pseudonymous blog about interpersonal relationships based her interactions as a hotel clerk, decided to say "Good day" at every possible opportunity for the rest of her life.

"Words matter," Melinda-Joy whispered, without meaning to, and hoped that the guest had not heard.

To Melinda-Joy, The Serial Stowaway said that a room had been reserved for her under the name Clarissa Clarke.

After tapping her keyboard and consulting her screen, Melinda-Joy swiveled her attention back to the woman behind the sunglasses, confirming a two-night stay, the bill for which was on the master account of—she glanced back at the screen and resumed with not a whit of discernible irony—Stunning Productions. Melinda-Joy would only, she continued, need Ms. Clarke's identification and a credit card to have on file for incidentals. However, as she was uttering the last syllable of that request, Melinda-Joy glanced one more time at the screen, and corrected herself. Stunning Productions, Melinda-Joy said in the tone one might say "Happy Birthday" to her best friend, was covering all incidentals as well, so the credit card would not be necessary. That was some A-list treatment, she thought.

"But," Melinda-Joy added, "I will need your identification." In her training, Melinda-Joy had been instructed to use "we" rather than "I," but a superseding personal code held that she was a singular and not a plural when it came to her employment.

The Serial Stowaway nodded and from her tote withdrew

the pummeled papers she had acquired on the airplane. Placing them on the insufficient counter space, she smoothed them with the edge of her hand and glanced across the counter at Melinda-Joy's name tag, grateful that she was able to read it through her sunglasses.

"Melinda-Joy," The Serial Stowaway confided, "I'm afraid I've had quite a day. My agent has botched my bio in the most insulting way, the airline lost my luggage, I am dreading the ridiculous television show I have agreed to appear on, and I have misplaced my wallet. I hope, Melinda-Joy, that this letter and itinerary from the show's producer—which includes my name and this hotel stay—will do for identification."

It was a nice point. The policy of D'accord Resort and Spa, as vetted and approved by its owner, the far larger Harrington Hotels, which in turn was owned by a holding company recently rebranded as Vigorance (a first step in its transformation into an operating company with an integrated, synergistic portfolio) was to require identification for all guests. However, it was not a legal requirement, and from time to time, legitimate guests did not possess traditional identification. Which alternate form of identification to accept was at the discretion of front desk clerks of certain rank, and it just so happened that Melinda-Joy's new rank of Assistant Front Desk Manager was one of those ranks.

Melinda-Joy took in The Serial Stowaway. This woman's neutral demeanor belied her story of a harried day. Her sunglasses were crooked enough to suggest they were not hers. Her hat was askew in a way that no one used to wearing such a hat would tolerate, and anyway the band still had a tag attached.

The Serial Stowaway was continuing. "Perhaps sometime in the past you would have recognized me—Clarissa Clarke, Lewis and Clarke—but I'm afraid those days are gone."

Melinda-Joy smiled and, in a tone friendly and impersonal enough to serve as a model in Front Desk Clerk training, said "Of course I remember you, Ms. Clarke," and tapped the keys to make a room assignment. As she handed the paper fold containing the room key across the counter to The Serial Stowaway, Melinda-Joy saw her supervisor in her peripheral vision. The words that matter, Melinda-Joy thought, were, "Fuck you, Mr. Scarf Man."

As The Serial Stowaway and Melinda-Joy parted company, a man and woman were joining the now-longer line of guests waiting to register. The woman, whose gray hair was in a striking side-swept style, gesticulated as she spoke. The man nodded along with an enthusiasm that emphasized his jutting jaw and proud bouffant.

On her way to the elevator, The Serial Stowaway saw an easel-supported, foam-mounted sign that read "AXIOM Annual Summit, Breakout Rooms," with an arrow pointing down an empty hallway. Removing her sunglasses, The Serial Stowaway saw just a few feet down the hall a solitary table with a solitary tray holding a picked-through pile of chocolate chip cookies. The Serial Stowaway approached the table, wrapped three cookies in a paper napkin with the Axiom logo, put the package into her tote, then retreated to the main corridor and on to her elevator bank. In her room, she double locked the door, not out of any special danger or fear, but because double-locking a door is a minimal prerequisite for combating the continuous vulnerability of life.

The buttons and levers on the shower in The Serial Stowaway's bathroom came right to the edge of prohibitively confounding, and the water, when it finally emerged, was itself strange, mimicking as it did a light rain falling straight down from above, but the temperature was lovely and the supplied shampoo and shower gel smelled like spearmint, which was The Serial Stowaway's favorite flavor of gum when she was a child.

As The Serial Stowaway showered, five floors below, at the registration desk, Clarissa Clarke, Francis November at her elbow looking ready to be helpful, was at high volume insisting on her bona fides across a counter to a man with a ridiculous red silk scarf and a suited young man who was actually trembling, clearly not cut out for the hospitality business, especially in L.A. Next to the trembling young man stood Melinda-Joy, whose face read delight in a manner so benign as to never be actionable.

The red-scarved man, pointing to the computer screen, gave orders to the trembling young man, spluttered obsequiousness to Clarissa and secondarily to Francis, and, having been given a description of the impersonator by a reluctant Melinda-Joy, raised his finger in a way that usually accompanies the proclamation "tally ho," and stalked off.

Clarissa sighed and said, "What more could happen?" Francis smiled reassuringly in a way that had cooled the fires of far better known and more eruptive celebrities, as Melinda-Joy stepped back to her station, lifted her telephone receiver, and pushed a three-button room extension.

The Serial Stowaway had just finished dressing when the phone rang.

Ninety seconds later, in the fifth-floor hallway of the D'accord Resort and Spa, the doors to an upward-heading elevator and the doors to a downward-heading elevator opened at the same time. This act of fate allowed for the red-scarved man, emerging from the former, to see The Serial Stowaway entering the latter. The time elapsed before both doors closed was sufficient to allow the red-scarved man to step in front of the opening to the downward elevator, but not to find words or actions to stop The Serial Stowaway, who, recognizing by his outraged expression that the red-scarved man was her pursuer and wanting to assuage his angst, gave the poor man a polite smile and finger-wave as the door panels drew together.

Back on the lobby level, The Serial Stowaway made a sharp left to the breakout session hallway. She was out of sight by the time the red-scarved man returned to the registration area to retrieve Melinda-Joy for aid in finding the interloper, going so far as to grasp her elbow, an act he thought better of when Melinda-Joy calmly requested that he remove his hand before she cut it off, reported him to H.R., or both.

In the hallway, The Serial Stowaway reached for the lever to the first door past the now-further-depleted cookie tray, which opened into the Miami Suite. For fifteen minutes or so, she sat in on a session titled "ROI in the Fast Lane: Implementing Scalable Plans to Maximize Investment in the Digital Era." Moving down the hall to the New Orleans Suite, she spent ten minutes in "Keep Up or Lose Out: Upskilling for Al in the Digital Era." Next, she entered the Houston Suite, for "From Silos to Synergy: Enhancing Success Through Team Collaboration in Zero-Trust Networks." She stayed in this session until its conclusion, both because only two other people were in the audience and she felt bad for the presenter, whose voice was quavering, and because at one point the door behind her opened, and the red-scarved man stuck his head in and looked around.

With a slide on the screen behind him pleading, "QUESTIONS?" the presenter, hearing none, allowed with evident gratitude the session to conclude. The Serial Stowaway accepted a business card from the presenter and reentered the hallway. By now, it was empty. Even the cookie tray had been removed.

The semi-sprawling layout of the D'accord Resort and Spa—featuring tropical-resort–style outdoor pool with secluded poolside cabanas and adjacent hot tub, ESCALATE Fitness Center overlooking the pool, Top Star Spa, D-Club Lounge, two three-star restaurants, and business center with six semi-private cubicles—gave The Serial Stowaway a sufficient landscape to roam and a chance of avoiding discovery by the red-scarved man. Especially appreciated was the stylish seclusion of the D'accord Resort and Spa pool area, offering a blissful retreat from the outside world, where The Serial Stowaway was even able to sneak in a nap.

With evening pressing in, running out of places to explore in D'accord, and having a while back burned through any energy provided by the complimentary chocolate chip cookies, The Serial Stowaway spotted at the end of an otherwise deserted corridor a handful of brightly attired bodies. Retrieving her broad brimmed hat from her tote and replacing it on her head, The Serial Stowaway approached, finding herself outside the Pinnacle Ballroom, which a glance from the hallway showed to be full of round tables with seating sufficient for perhaps two hundred, although only roughly half of the seats appeared to be occupied. Ten or so people—women in vibrant gowns, men in dark suits—were holding glasses of various sizes and shapes, and to one side was a sign that read "AXIOM Awards Banquet. Private, Ticketed Event."

With murmurs and sighs expressing their feelings about entering the ballroom, the hallway gathering began to make its way past the somewhat less elegantly clothed and badge-wearing staff obviously eager to close the door. The Serial Stowaway followed the group and heard behind her one staff person commenting on the discrepancy between the number of invitees and the number of people who had actually shown up. "Last day of the conference, what did they expect?" the voice said, sounding less disappointed and more satisfied with being proven correct.

Inside, The Serial Stowaway paused to let her eyes adjust to the darkness, that process hampered by the brightness of a huge screen announcing the name of the event against some sort of undulating amoeba-like shapes. After cruising the perimeter twice, The Serial Stowaway found a seat roughly in the middle of the room at a table occupied by three bread baskets, six glasses of water with nearly melting ice, and one person—an intense woman studying the contents of a three-ring binder. In front of The Serial Stowaway was a place setting of silverware and red cloth napkin and a paper placemat that, amid colorful pictures of award statuettes and bursting fireworks, had these words:

Let's celebrate the winners!

Welcome to the AXIOM Annual Awards Banquet

AXIOM: Helping companies elevate performance by acquiring insights, accelerating decisions, and advancing targets to transform visions into an integrated reality.

Allowing her eyes to swim around the room, The Serial Stowaway saw that the huge screen she had noted previously was stretched across the back of a stage on which rested a clear plexiglass lectern and a long table holding in neat alignment at least fifty silver statuettes, assaying out, The Serial Stowaway calculated, to about one statuette for every two guests.

Feeling a presence at her side, The Serial Stowaway found her placemat being covered by a plate of sauce-covered chicken breast, green beans, crinkle-cut carrots, and potato chunks, along with a separate plate of green salad.

The Serial Stowaway removed and stowed her hat—her good manners were from instinct more than experience but were dependable nonetheless—and gratefully began to eat, noticing as she did that the intense woman had moved her plate to one side and was continuing to study her binder.

As The Serial Stowaway ate, people appeared on the stage—a man with a proud midriff and a woman whose slightness threatened to be overwhelmed by an elaborately draped gold gown. The man stepped to the lectern, leaned toward the stick microphone, and peered not at his audience or his onstage companion, but at what to The Serial Stowaway was a black rectangle set on the foot of the stage. As he began to speak, The Serial Stowaway noticed that her tablemate was mouthing the words along with him.

By the time opening remarks had been remarked and three awards had been given—the James M. Muldave Project of the Year Award, the Gerome A. Smyth Innovation Award, and the Jennifer L. Timore Service Award, the names of awards and recipients (at least three per award) flashed on the screen, the statuettes handed out the recipients by the gowned woman, and the recipients exited without any acceptance speeches, The Serial Stowaway's tablemate mouthing each syllable as it was uttered from the stage—dinner plates had been retrieved and deserts had been deposited in their place.

Between each award, The Serial Stowaway had glanced toward the entrance in case the red-scarved man would track her to this unlikely location. When people had sampled their desserts and accepted or rejected coffee, the handsomely girthed man gestured for the gold-gowned woman to return to the lectern, and The Serial Stowaway's tablemate turned to the next page in her binder. As the tablemate mouthed along, the woman, eyes on the black box, spoke:

"There are so many more awards to come. I know you're especially eager for the Frank W. Sarnow Corporate Citizen of the Year Award and the Jason S. Tarnoff Lifetime Achievement Award. Don't worry, they're coming soon. But now, it's time for us to sit back, enjoy our desserts and coffee, and take a few minutes to listen, laugh, and reflect." She paused, eyes sweeping the audience because she had been told during rehearsal to make eye contact.

"This year, we've gathered in Los Angeles, show business capital of the world. And so, we thought we would inject a little star power into this very special evening." Here she took a deep breath, having been warned that there would be hell to pay from the speakers' bureau if the keynote's bio was not delivered precisely as written, fixed her eyes intently on the black rectangle, and gripped the edges of the lectern.

"We are thrilled to be joined now by a gentleman who for many years has been at the epicenter of all things glittering and glamorous here in L.A. He has worked shoulder to shoulder as publicist and confidant to shining stars from Jennifer Lopez to Barbra Streisand, from Beyonce to Ray Romano." Another deep breath. Having practiced the script diligently, she knew the next sentences were mouthfuls.

"Not long ago, tonight's speaker left the trenches of Tinseltown to become an in-demand celebrity watcher whom you have surely seen sharing his wit and wisdom on the Red Carpets of your favorite award-show broadcasts. And even more recently, our guest transformed the lessons in grit, graciousness, and gravitas that he learned from his celebrity clients into a fabulously successful life coaching business…and into his just-released book *Love Yourself and other Life Lessons from the Glitterati*. Now," the script indicated a pause, "please join me in welcoming this evening's very special guest," the script indicated a pause, "Francis November!" (Her stage directions read: Lead applause. Shake hands with speaker. Exit to audience.)

In the audience, The Serial Stowaway's tablemate pushed her binder aside and reached with one hand for her spoon and with the other for her peanut butter mousse, as from backstage, waving and smiling broadly, entered The Serial Stowaway's former airplane seatmate, his bouffant bouncing with his stride, the white of his teeth complementing the white of the notecards in his left hand, his right hand extended to shake the hand of his introducer.

With thanks for allowing him to be the evening's infotainment—an enfant terrible grin accented that word—Francis made eye contact with three members of the audience in three different sections of the room, consulted a notecard, and began.

The presentation was divided into five parts, each brief—he only had 20 minutes—and each helpfully illustrated with a slide and photos of the relevant celebrities. With a few more self-conscious chuckles than one might expect from a person so often on television, Francis led the audience through the first four of his categories of celebrity life lessons:

Pursue your passion…but don't obsess (examples: Madonna, Justin Bieber).

It's OK to be vulnerable…sometimes (examples: Queen Latifa, Ben Affleck).

Focus on your body…and your soul (examples: Jennifer Lopez, Jim Carrey).

Listen…but don't let the critics get you down (examples: Cher, Lady Gaga).

Say what you will about his occasional nervous laughs, Francis November had one orator's skill firmly in hand: he made regular, unhurried, and sincere eye contact with people throughout the audience. This skill went a long way toward keeping almost everyone off their phones and attending to him as he strolled the stage, notecards in left hand, right hand free for broad gestures to drive home key points.

Consulting the countdown clock on the foot of the stage next to the teleprompter screen and noting he had five minutes remaining, Francis headed into the final and in his view the most important life lesson.

"Love yourself," he proclaimed, then hesitated dramatically, "and your brand."

The slide showed a photo montage of Barbra Streisand— in *Funny Girl*, in *What's Up, Doc*, in *Yentl*.

Again, Francis paused, but this pause extended beyond dramatic effect. Francis looked at a spot he hadn't looked at all evening—his feet. The audience seemed to shift en mass in its seats, except for The Serial Stowaway, who, having recently looked behind her to see if the red-scarved man or any uniformed person who seemed bent on pursuit had entered the room, was settled comfortably, looking at Francis with no more than moderate curiosity.

Francis brought his head up and, gazing into an undifferentiated part of the audience, continued. "Here," he said, "is where I usually start with one of my favorite stories about Babs." He gestured behind him at the screen. Well, her friends call her Babs. I always called her Ms. Streisand. The story I was going to tell was about the time Barbra found out that on iPhones, Siri was mispronouncing her last name, and so she called Apple CEO Tim Cook and asked him to fix it. Which he did. But there is another Barbra story that I've never told, that I've never known how to fit into this talk, but it has always tugged at me. And I think tonight is the time to tell it." He looked at The Serial Stowaway and away, almost as if embarrassed.

"This happened while Barbra was working on the script for *Yentl*. Barbra was having a conversation with the novelist Chaim Potok, who had offered some ideas for the script, about her time studying with Lee Strasberg, who didn't pay her much attention, and in the middle of the story she interrupted herself and started a different story. Here is what she said, as I recall it." Again, he glanced toward The Serial Stowaway.

"Barbara said, 'When I was fifteen, I remember seeing people, if they pretended to be something they were not, and thinking they were nothing. But if people, even if they were nothing much—I mean, no charisma, no particular aura—if they just were themselves, if they were just being, well, nothing, then I found them fascinating, just by being human. Once they acted, it was false. They were their inadequacies. But once they were just nothing, they were something.'"

Francis went on. "I've never repeated that story, but I

think about it. It's an attractive notion, the idea of being important by being unimportant. I suppose we all try to project an image of ourselves that corrects what we perceive as our inadequacies.

"The problem with the idea, I think, is this: What if you don't try to be something special, what if you don't try to be someone fascinating? What happens? I'll tell you what happens, in Hollywood, anyway, and probably everywhere. What happens is that you are ignored. Completely and universally ignored." He seemed surprised that he still held his note cards and put them into his back pocket.

"So that was the problem with that anecdote. As clever and insightful as it sounded, it seemed flawed, and so I didn't use it in my speeches or my book. But I thought about that comment of Barbra's, on my flight here this morning from New York. I was sitting in the window seat—it was a three-seat arrangement—and I was having a delightful conversation with Clarissa Clarke, former member of the comedy team Lewis and Clarke, who is in town to take part in a show called *D-Listed*. And she was talking about her career, and I was talking about celebrities the way I do, and we were having a great time. But here's the thing." Another embarrassed pause. "In the middle seat was another person, a woman, I don't know how old, I don't guess at women's ages, I've spent too much time in show business to make that mistake. Anyway, this woman didn't introduce herself, and I didn't introduce myself to her, and Clarissa Clarke didn't introduce herself. And we just talked across this person in the middle seat for pretty much the entire flight, talked across her like she wasn't even there.

"And while we were talking, I was paying attention to the conversation, but I was also thinking about Barbra's observation, and I was thinking, well, here is someone—the woman in the middle seat—who is not saying a word, who is certainly not acting important. And you know, I thought, in one way Barbra was exactly right. This person, not saying anything, she certainly wasn't a strong physical presence, you know what I mean? In one way she was nothing. And the more I thought about her, and have continued to think about her, by being nothing, she was something."

Almost as if interrupting himself, Francis said, just shy of a shout, "But." He shook his head and in a quieter voice continued. "But, what was the result of her being herself, of her not acting, of her being something, being someone important and special? I'll tell you the result. The result was that I totally, arrogantly, rudely ignored her. Clarissa Clarke and I treated her as if she were invisible, as if she were nothing."

Francis looked at the countdown clock, which was at zero and flashing. In the teleprompter screen, the script had been replaced by one word, all in capital letters: "CLOSE."

"OK, fine, I'm out of time, and I don't want to be rude to all of you, but I have a reason for bringing all this up." He glanced searchingly toward the back of the room. "Could someone bring up the house lights? Is that possible? The reason I tell that story is that this evening, in the audience…ah," he said, as the house lights glowed softly, "there we go, thank you…in the audience, tonight, I see is the very woman I was speaking about. The woman in the middle seat, the woman who, in the words of Barbra Streisand, by being nothing is truly something."

Eyes firmly planted on The Serial Stowaway, Francis November gestured toward her, as if offering his hand for her to hold.

"Would you please stand, madam? I would like to publicly apologize, and I would like everyone in this room to give you a round of applause because you are not invisible. You are somebody special."

The Serial Stowaway sensed that the audience, some of whom were pointing their phones toward her, wanted to applaud but would not until she stood, and she further realized that Mr. November would not be able to complete his presentation until she stood, and that the winners of remaining awards would not receive their statuettes or accolades until she stood, and these people would not be able to go back to their rooms until she stood, and it would just be discourteous for her not to stand. So, she stood.

As she prepared to rise, before the applause began, and before Francis concluded his speech, and before the winners of the Frank W. Sarnow Corporate Citizen of the Year Award and the Jason S. Tarnoff Lifetime Achievement Award were announced and feted, and before the audience was able to stand on creaky legs and consider whether they had energy enough for some L.A. nightlife, there was a second of silence.

That silence was broken by a voice, a loud voice, a voice constituted of one-third surprise, one-third anger, and one-third righteousness, a voice that said, "THERE SHE IS!"

It didn't matter that The Serial Stowaway got away. It didn't matter that the side door led her to a back-of-house hallway that looked like the corridor of an old hospital, lined with, instead of gurneys, tables of leftover food (The Serial Stowaway grabbed some rolls) and rolling bins half-filled with linens and white-garbed workers who seemed interested in but not committed to the sight of The Serial Stowaway walking briskly down the hallway and, thirty seconds later, the red-scarved, purple-faced man (who had left Melinda-Joy behind in the banquet hall where she was enjoying an uneaten peanut butter mousse and muttering, "Words matter"), pushing aside bins and people as he ran the same path. It didn't matter that The Serial Stowaway pushed through a door that led into another hotel hallway and blazed a path so confoundingly circuitous that at one point while riding an escalator up she passed the red-scarved man going down, giving the man a smile and finger wave. It didn't matter that The Serial Stowaway boarded a shuttle for the airport or that the shuttle was pulling away when the red-scarved man reached it, shaking his fist and shouting. It didn't matter that The Serial Stowaway traversed unmolested the TSA checkpoint at the Los Angeles International Airport, slept undisturbed in terminal three, in the morning surreptitiously returned the broad-brimmed hat and sunglasses to Hollywood Style, and successfully snuck onto a morning flight to Chicago.

It didn't matter because, once back in the O'Hare Airport, The Serial Stowaway stopped at a newsstand to see if any of the celebrities Mr. November mentioned were on the covers of any of the magazines arrayed on the racks, and when she resumed her stroll down the corridor, she was recognized by a woman named Amanda monitoring nine closed-circuit TV screens in a tiny room, who, feeling a pang of reluctance because she rather admired The Serial Stowaway, alerted airport security, which took her into custody and turned over to the Chicago police at the airport, who arrested her for loitering, and took her to the Chicago Police Department's Sixteenth District Station, from which she was transported by van to the Cook County Jail.

Perhaps, The Serial Stowaway thought, from jail she would write a letter to Mr. November, thanking him for his thoughtful words.

Chapter 8:
The Serial Stowaway
and the Jailhouse Interview

In a complex of buildings on South California Avenue in Chicago called the Cook County Jail by most Chicagoans, the Hotel California by those who knew it more intimately, and the Cook County Department of Corrections by the Cook County Sheriff when addressing the public, resting on ninety-six acres constituting eight city blocks, one of the current nine thousand two hundred and one detainees, a sixty-three-year-old woman known in the media as The Serial Stowaway, sat, a beige telephone handset held to her ear, in a small, square room.

The Serial Stowaway heard several clicks and then a bored voice saying, "This call is recorded and subject to monitoring." After a pause and the sound of furry silence, the voice continued, "Call accepted."

Probably, The Serial Stowaway thought, the man on the other end of the line had heard this also.

The governing motif of the 150-square-foot room in

which The Serial Stowaway sat might be viewed as *erasure*: beige glazed cinderblock walls with a few black smudges testifying to decades of mostly successful weekly scrubbing, an unstained beechnut plank table subjected to repeated scouring jobs that had managed to obliterate most of the words and symbols carved into its top surface, an acoustic tile ceiling, punctured here and there, covering whatever pipes and ductwork that kept the building habitable, and two unstained armless beechnut chairs with schoolhouse backs designed to remove any comfort one might feel in the act of sitting. One of two chairs had been placed in the corner nearest the door, and the polyester white top and khaki slacks of the woman sitting in it did the job of eliminating individuality that was the purpose of every uniform, aided in this case by the expressionless face of a stout woman, whose complexion was a good match for the color of the walls, the beechnut, and the peel-and-stick tile that erased the concrete floor beneath. Even the telephone furthered the erasure motif, its face being a flat plastic surface where buttons—and, in past years, a dial—would normally be.

Of course, erasure is a metaphor, and a metaphor is a point of view, and it did not happen to be The Serial Stowaway's point of view.

To The Serial Stowaway, the largely blank walls gave prominence to the vague black smudges, perhaps vestiges of words, perhaps of doodles, but less interesting in their denotation than in the randomness of their shapes.

To The Serial Stowaway, the subtle indentations of the tabletop seemed some form of braille.

To The Serial Stowaway, the seat of the armless chairs, when explored by curious fingertips, yielded indentations that one might imagine as gulleys in an otherwise rolling plane.

To The Serial Stowaway, the punctures added the sound-absorbing holes designed into the ceiling tile might, with very little effort, be imagined as caused by ball point pens tossed up by bored attorneys or police detectives or corrections staff.

Even the button-less phone, to The Serial Stowaway, was not an erasure but a revelation. What an honor to be one of so few citizens to slide her fingers across the smooth surface that would only exist when no buttons were allowed to intrude on its perfection.

And then there was Celeste. Smooth-faced Celeste. Featureless Celeste. Expressionless Celeste. Celeste was The Serial Stowaway's friend, a friendship discerned by a crinkle at the corner of Celeste's eye, the twitch at one corner of her lips, the hint of elevation of one eyebrow, none of which would be visible if not against an otherwise blank facial backdrop.

As for The Serial Stowaway, her relationship with the motif of erasure was rather complex. In the washed-out blue V-neck scrubs provided to women (men wore beige) by Cook County, her body type unremarkable, The Serial Stowaway all but blended into the walls and furniture to the point of disappearing altogether. Even her gray-now-nearing-white hair, a contrast in color to her surroundings, contributed to The Serial Stowaway's erasure in its unremarkable bob cut and, more especially, the societally conditioned expectation that the gray hair of age signaled a capability of thought heading toward inoperability and a presence in the world in the process of fading to nothing.

Although The Serial Stowaway fit the impression of erasure yielded by a cursory scan of the room, she also fit into the view of the room as The Serial Stowaway perceived it. As the faint black smudges were to the otherwise scrubbed wall, and as the faint symbols were to the otherwise scoured tabletop, so was The Serial Stowaway's barely perceptible smile to the otherwise innocuousness of her mien. That is to say, it was some combination of a code, a work of art, and a faint memory.

"Jane?" Even this one word heard by The Serial Stowaway in the telephone receiver revealed the practiced timber and enunciation of a male on-camera investigative reporter: mellifluous with a hint of gravel.

After receiving the journalist's letter, The Serial Stowaway had watched one of his segments on the local news, broadcast from a television mounted out of easy reach in the intersection of walls and ceiling of the recreation room. She did not remember the topic of his report, but had been struck by his hair—wavy, lightly gelled, salt-and-pepper, combed straight back and, visible when he was shown at an angle, in the back flapping raffishly past his collar—and even more by his teeth, which were whiter than his starched white shirt, which he wore without a necktie, unlike his male colleagues on the broadcast, meant to suggest a certain energetic unconventionality. The Serial Stowaway had noticed in her airplane travels that most people's teeth were rarely and minimally visible, a wide-open mouth being required to pull the lips back far enough and for long enough duration to display teeth. In contrast, this reporter, whose name was Ed Byrnes, either naturally or through long practice managed to display his teeth continuously. Or perhaps they were just so white that even when they peeked out from between his lips they stole the show.

"Yes," The Serial Stowaway replied. She extended the "e" into what may have been an attempt to sound like a more elderly lady than she was or may have been just a catch in her voice from the chronically dry air.

Byrnes: Hello, this is Ed. Ed Byrnes.

Serial Stowaway: Hello, Edwin.

Byrnes: Um, hello, how are you?

Serial Stowaway: I'm fine. How are you?

Byrnes: I'm fine as well, thank you for asking. Well—

Serial Stowaway: You're welcome.

Byrnes: Yes, well, thank you, um, Jane. May I call you Jane?

Serial Stowaway: That's what they call me around here. Yes, of course. I like the sound of your voice saying anything, really.

Byrnes: Thank you, and—

Serial Stowaway: I'm afraid I called you Edwin without asking your permission. May I?

Byrnes: Call me by my first name? Yes. Jane, may I record

this call?

Serial Stowaway (chuckling): Well, Edwin, if you heard the voice before our call started, it seems that someone is already recording us.

Byrnes: Ah. Ha. Yes, I, of course. But I doubt I have access to that recording. This is for my use. I have a recorder here, a nice one that the station gives me. I'll use this record to make sure I'm accurate when I write my script. And I'm sure we'll use a few clips of your voice on the air. But I haven't pushed the record button yet. Would it be OK if I do that?

Serial Stowaway: Is the button red?

Byrnes: Um, yes, as a matter of fact it is. I suppose most record buttons are red, now that I think of it.

Serial Stowaway: Good. Then please do push the red button.

Byrnes: All right, I've started recording. Now Jane, I know you have been reluctant to speak to the press in the past. And I'm honored that you have chosen to break your silence with me. And I wonder: why now, and why with me?

Serial Stowaway: Well, Edwin, that really was a nice letter you wrote me.

Byrnes: Thank you, Jane.

Serial Stowaway: Also, Edwin, I watched one of your broadcasts, which was excellent.

Byrnes: Thank you. Much appreciated. Was it the most recent one? About the auto repair scams? Yes, I thought that one came out well. But why speak out at all, and why now after, what, almost twenty-five years as, well, as the media says, a serial stowaway?

Serial Stowaway (shrugging): Oh, I just shrugged, but I guess you couldn't see that. You know, when people shrug it can mean so many things. But because you can't see me, I suppose I'll need to put my shrug in words. Let's see, this shrug meant, "It's hard to explain."

Byrnes: I see. Well, could you try, try to explain?

Serial Stowaway: Aside from your persuasiveness, which is considerable in writing, and now that we are speaking, you have just the loveliest voice, I feel even more per-suaded. But I have to tell you that there was another per-son who influenced my decision. A man recently gave me this piece of advice, and that advice was, "Be curious." And I thought, what am I curious about? And, here in jail, I thought, I'm curious what it would be like to not take my airplane trips. And then your letter came, and I thought, I will tell this man that I will never take another of my airplane trips, and that will commit me.

Byrnes: I see, and—

Serial Stowaway: Another piece of advice the man gave me was, "Show interest in others so they will show inter-est in you." I just mention that because I suppose in your work you show interest in others all the time, although perhaps it's not so important that they show interest in you because you're the reporter, not the subject.

Byrnes: So, Jane, are you pledging to us here, exclusively, that you will never take another airplane trip without an authorized ticket?

Serial Stowaway: I am.

Byrnes: Well, thank you, Jane, for having that kind of trust in me, in us.

Serial Stowaway: Certainly, Edgar.

Byrnes: Um, now perhaps we can go all the way to the beginning.

Serial Stowaway (singing): It's a very good place to start.

Byrnes: What's that? Oh, yes, I get it, "Do-Re-Mi." Yes, very good.

Serial Stowaway: I always loved that song. Don't you? I love every song in *The Sound of Music*. Except maybe "The Lonely Goatherd." I could have done without that one. I used to play the record of *The Sound of Music* over and over when I was a child. Except "The Lonely Goatherd." I don't want to be mean, but that song was simply not pleasant. Sometimes I would lift the phonograph arm and skip right over that song. It was the first song on the second side. I felt a little bad about doing that. After all, many people worked very hard on that song. But, Edgar, life is just too short to listen to a song that you don't particularly like. Don't you agree?

The Serial Stowaway did not explain to Ed—whose full first name was neither Edwin nor Edgar—that, although she loved the songs before "The Lonely Goatherd," and although she loved the songs after "The Lonely Goatherd," she loved even more the care, the precision, even the courage that it took, after turning the record over to side two, to shift the tone arm to the left, pausing at just the point where the needle hovered above the narrow, ungrooved strip of vinyl that indicated the division between "The Lonely Goatherd" and "The Sound of Music," and to bring the tone arm down slowly, not wanting the needle to damage the record, not sure if the needle would land in precisely the right spot, but finally bracing herself to let the needle come down and find out what would happen.

Byrnes: I quite agree. Quite. But, well, back to the very beginning, can you tell us about the very first time you boarded a flight without a ticket?

Serial Stowaway (shrugging): I've shrugged again, Edgar. This time the shrug meant, "Why not?" Let's see, the first flight I took was to Paris. Oh, it was so beautiful. The lights, the cafes, the people.

Byrnes: OK. Yes, Paris is beautiful.

Serial Stowaway: Have you been there?

Byrnes: I have not, but I've heard it's beautiful. Um, Jane, OK. Let's go even further back. Back really to the beginning. Can you tell me about your family? About your life growing up?

Serial Stowaway: Well, as I mentioned, my mother was a big fan of *The Sound of Music*.

Byrnes: OK.

Serial Stowaway: And she was very attentive to numbers.

Byrnes: Good with numbers? Was she a mathematician?

Serial Stowaway: I don't know if she was good with numbers. She paid attention to numbers. She had her favorite numbers, and she paid attention to them.

Byrnes: Um, OK, Jane, could I ask you a question I know our viewers are very curious about, and I am too. How do you do it? How do you get past all the security we have at airports these days? TSA, then actually getting past the agent taking boarding passes? Do you get a ticket or a boarding pass from somewhere?

Serial Stowaway: No, I don't.

Byrnes: Well, maybe I should ask that a different way. Where do you get your ideas for how to stow away?

Serial Stowaway: Where do I get my ideas?

Byrnes: Yes.

Serial Stowaway: Well, I think of them.

Byrnes: I guess what I'm asking is do you have a plan each time you, well, each time you stow away? And what is that plan?

Serial Stowaway: I do have a plan, Edgar. I plan to take an airplane ride.

Byrnes: But I mean take it down one level. What are the components? What are the steps?

Serial Stowaway (shrugging): I have shrugged again, Edgar. I believe this shrug means, "That is a very hard question, but I will try to answer it." My plan, Edgar, is that I watch what happens and then I do something and then I watch what happens. Like that, again and again.

Byrnes: You do something.

Serial Stowaway: I do something.

Byrnes: And you watch what happens?

Serial Stowaway: I watch what happens.

Byrnes: Well, um, do you have any help? You know, like getting past security? Does somebody help you?

Serial Stowaway: People are so helpful, don't you agree? But Edgar, surely you don't want me to get anyone in trouble.

Byrnes: I suppose not.

Serial Stowaway: I should think not.

Byrnes: Perhaps we could come at this from a different direction. Another question our viewers have—and my producers and I have discussed this not only among ourselves but with, um, professionals—is why you do it? Why do you take these trips?

Serial Stowaway: I'm afraid I am going to need you to explain that question for me.

Byrnes: Sure. Well, as I think about it, you may be traveling from something. By that I mean you may be trying to get away from something. Fleeing. Or, flight, as it were. Is that how you feel when you take one of your trips?

Serial Stowaway: Let me be sure I understand. Once I met a young man on a plane who was not wearing socks who was leaving a city where he was afraid of losing his job. Is that what you mean by traveling from something? Perhaps that's a poor example for you, Edgar. I'm sure you would never get fired.

Byrnes: OK, let's try another possible reason for stowing away. Are you, perhaps, traveling toward something? Going somewhere? Trying to get to some destination?

Serial Stowaway: Well, I think everyone on the airplane is going to where that airplane is going.

Byrnes: Well, let me say this a different way. First, maybe you're afraid and need to leave someplace. Or, second, maybe you feel a compulsion to get to another place.

Serial Stowaway: Are those two my only options?

Byrnes: Those are the ones I can think of.

Serial Stowaway (after glancing toward Celeste, who unfortunately could hear only The Serial Stowaway's side of the conversation): I promise, Edgar, to give that question my most serious consideration. I'm sorry, is your name Edgar? Edwin? Edward?

Byrnes: It's Edward, actually.

Serial Stowaway: Oh, that's wonderful! Like Edward Kennedy! Did you ever interview him?

Byrnes: I did not, unfortunately.

Serial Stowaway: Once, when I had flown to Washington, D.C., this was not long before his death, I met Senator Kennedy. At least I am under the impression that I met him. I was walking on Constitution Avenue, I remember it was spring, and a man who looked very much like Senator Kennedy, he was wearing a dark suit, appeared at my side almost as if from nowhere. He walked along with me for, oh, maybe a full minute. Finally, he said, "I will rent a tuxedo, and somebody will buy me a drink," or something similar. Because I didn't understand, I said to him, "Words matter, Senator, and I didn't understand yours." I took the next path to the right, because I wasn't sure that conversation was going anywhere, and from there I went to the airport. Perhaps that is what you mean about wanting to get away, Edward?

Ed Byrnes did not immediately reply, being struck by that phrase "Words matter," liking the sound of it, rolling it around on his tongue and lips, and in his mind.

Serial Stowaway: Edward? Are you there?

Byrnes: I'm sorry. Now Jane, one question I'd like to ask is a little sensitive. But here goes. Have you ever been diagnosed with any sort of emotional or mental disorder? Are you bipolar, for example?

Serial Stowaway: No, Edward. I'm good.

Byrnes: You're good?

Serial Stowaway: I'm good.

Byrnes: I suppose you are. Which reminds me of another question: What do you think of other famous, um, let's see, impostors—like, say, Frank Abagnale. They made a movie about him. Or do you compare yourself to escape artists like Harry Houdini?

Serial Stowaway: Edward, I was under the impression that the subject of this interview was me, not these other people.

Byrnes: Of course. Of course. So, to wrap up, how many flights have you taken without benefit of a ticket?

Serial Stowaway: I would say thirty.

Byrnes: And your most recent one was…?

Serial Stowaway: From Los Angeles to Chicago.

Byrnes: And that flight will be your last unauthorized flight? You will never take another one…unless you have a ticket?

Serial Stowaway: I promise you, Edward. Never again.

Byrnes: Well, this has been wonderfully insightful. Thank you very much for allowing us to have a glimpse inside your extremely unique life.

Before hanging up, The Serial Stowaway turned to look at Celeste, who shrugged so faintly that when her shoulders resumed their previous position, it was like they had never moved.

At the time of the interview, The Serial Stowaway had been in the Cook County Jail for one hundred and four days. Previously, she had served shorter stints in jails around the country, always on charges of trespassing rather than the federal charge of stowing away, before being released on probation, which she would violate by leaving the city, or being sent to voluntary residential mental health settings, which she would leave before any scheduled departure date.

The one hundred and four days stretched to one hundred and forty-four. During that time, Ed Byrnes reviewed the transcript of his interview with The Serial Stowaway, recorded supplementary interviews with law enforcement and mental health officials, and wrote background based on research about The Serial Stowaway's travels collected by what he thought of as "his newsroom team." The team thought of itself in different ways depending on each person's worldview, life experience, and feelings on any day.

Assembling the package to submit to the broadcast's editorial director, Ed felt satisfied, for the most part. In the vernacular of his business, The Serial Stowaway was a good get. But a good get gets you only so far. News reporters have a saying: hooking a fish takes a lot less skill than bringing it in. During the day, Ed was confident that he had brought in The Serial Stowaway. Hers was a compelling story. The script had come together nicely. He had The Serial Stowaway saying, "I'm good," which he placed in a context that made her seem to be bragging about her stowaway skills. He had her blaming her flights on a conspiracy involving Ted Kennedy. Most of all, he had her promising to never again stow away. That would be a solid kicker. He wasn't allowed to write copy for the news anchors, but he had drafted for the powers that be to consider a few intro and outro bullet points commenting on the exclusivity and high interest of the story and the rigor of the reporting. Still, some mornings he awoke before his alarm with a vestigial image of something insubstantial slipping through his fingers.

On the one hundred and forty-fifth day of her incarceration, The Serial Stowaway appeared before a great harrumphing judge who, in sentencing The Serial Stowaway to probation with electronic monitoring and transfer to what he called a transitional housing facility, commented that the justice system was ill-equipped to deal with people like The Serial Stowaway, people who were older, polite, and articulate, and who clearly had mental problems that caused them to be in conflict with the norms of society.

The Serial Stowaway was busy being moved into her room in the transitional housing facility, or was it transitional facility housing, a room so narrow that even someone of her limited stature could extend her arms and touch walls on either side, the evening Ed Byrnes' investigative report on her exploits was broadcast. The broadcast was, however, seen in the facility's living room by a few of her new housing-mates, who did not yet realize it pertained to their new co-resident.

The broadcast also was seen by a recreation room packed with The Serial Stowaway's recent jail-mates monitored by Celeste. The prisoners gave their reviews as the broadcast progressed, most expressing shock that so few lines spoken by The Serial Stowaway survived the cut. When the two anchors had, shaking their heads in admiration, congratulated Ed Byrnes for his "great work," and the broadcast had gone to a commercial for a burger chain that had recently slipped from the third to the fourth ranking among the region's fast-food offerings, one inmate's conclusion deftly summarized the critiques: "Clipped and spliced to nullity."

Celeste nodded so faintly that few realized her chin had dropped even one degree from the perpendicular.

The Cook County Sheriff's Department uses two types of global-position-system–enabled ankle monitors for those released under such supervision from the Cook County Jail. One type is active, sounding an alarm when the person wearing the device enters what is called an "exclusion zone." The other type is passive, displaying the location of the person at all times, but relying on a human to view the monitored person's location and to alert authorities if the monitored person is somewhere he or she should not be.

The Serial Stowaway's release was predicated on her having an active monitor that would sound an alarm if she left the transitional housing facility grounds, except for authorized outings, such as to visit her attorney. However, mistakes happen, especially in an environment as chaotic as the Cook County Jail, and the device placed on The Serial Stowaway was not an active but a passive monitor. Therefore, on the first morning The Serial Stowaway spent at the transitional facility, when one of the many screens at the Cook County Sheriff's Department Office in Rolling Meadows, Illinois, showed that The Serial Stowaway had left the facility, even if the human monitor had not been in the break room pouring coffee, he likely would not have noticed, from among all the dots on the various screens showing the people being monitored, that The Serial Stowaway was walking toward the nearest train station.

Similar rooms for the similar purpose of monitoring closed-circuit television feeds were located in the terminals of O'Hare Airport. Ninety-five minutes after The Serial Stowaway left the transitional facility, in a room containing twelve screens monitoring the output of terminal one's public cameras, Amanda, the weekday monitor for the past fifteen years, sat low in her swivel chair. She sat low because the chair itself was low to the ground and lower still because Amanda slumped in her seat, tired from last night's show for which she had booked a particularly persnickety group of standup comics, but at least the bar owner had allowed her, as a courtesy for being booker and emcee, to do a six-minute set rather than her usual five.

The timestamp on the upper left corner screen, which monitored the corridor housing gates C five through C twenty, showed a figure bent at the waist over a water fountain between a men's and women's restroom. Idly, Amanda watched the figure. When the head lifted from the fountain, it turned toward the camera, revealing a woman's face. The woman turned away from the camera, but then back. The woman brought up her hand, as though to wave, but brought it back down before making any gesture. She walked down the corridor, not quickly, not slowly, until out of the camera's view.

Amanda snorted. She had seen the news broadcast last night, including The Serial Stowaway's pledge to never again sneak onto a flight. And here she was. Amanda shook her head appreciatively and began formulating for her next standup set a routine about The Serial Stowaway. However, even at this early point in creating the routine, Amanda felt the weight of defeat because she was pretty sure the bit would take at least seven minutes to deliver.

Chapter 9:
The Serial Stowaway
and the Concluding Comments

Each day, the Atlanta-Hartsfield Airport, the busiest air hub in the United States, handles about two million arrivals and departures for almost three hundred thousand people. The airport handles these comings and goings with great efficiency, routinely ranking in the top five among airports with the fewest flight delays and cancellations.

However, any airport, especially one that handles such high volume, will experience some delays. Despite the best efforts and with the sincere regrets of well-trained and well-intentioned airport and airline personnel, some travelers will find themselves with time on their hands as they wait for flights promised to depart at a certain time to depart at some other time.

At eleven-forty on a Thursday night—alas, soon to be a Friday morning—one such traveler was a marketing executive named Rich Orlando. On his way home from a meeting with the company that had recently purchased his company,

Rich, sat on a stool at a counter between gate B-nineteen and a dark, gate-covered shop with a sign that said, "11 Alive Travel Store." Rich assumed that "11 Alive" was the name of an Atlanta television station, but he could not help thinking this an odd name for an airport vendor. Was this the shopping place for the eleven survivors of some flight gone horribly wrong?

Rich was not grumpy about the delay, nor did he welcome it. He was neither averse nor eager to reach his destination. This was a new state of mind for Rich. In the past, he had been eager about destinations. Lately, he found himself satisfied with wherever he happened to be.

A year ago, Rich had flown to Atlanta for a job interview, a job he sought more out of fear he was about to be fired from his current job than from desire to make a change. He had been nervous about everything, including the interview, so nervous he had even asked his gray-haired, innocuous female seatmate to help him rehearse. He had not gotten the job, but neither had he been fired. The company he interviewed with bought the company he worked for, and he had ended up with a modest raise, a new title, and more responsibility as some of his colleagues, including several who had seemed to be freezing Rich out, were terminated and Rich picked up various of their duties.

One of those duties was communication within the company—internal comms, as it was called. As a result, Rich, sitting at the counter in Atlanta-Hartsfield's B concourse, his laptop charging, was reading an article, emailed to him by the Chief Operating Officer as a good resource for his next task, titled "Mark Zuckerberg's Message to Laid-Off Facebook Employees Is a Masterclass in Good Leadership."

After checking Google for any update on his flight's departure time, Rich began playing with some wording for his company's announcement: "We are today embarking on a re-design of our non-client-serving teams, so that these teams can effectively support and scale with our firm as demand for our services continues to grow." He reread the sentence, decided he could work with that, but tomorrow. Letting his eyes drift around the concourse, he found himself counting the number of people within his view, which happened, he was pleased to note, to be eleven, including himself.

*

In his condominium on the near north side of Chicago, Ed Byrnes, recently laid off from his role as chief investigative reporter at the television station where he had worked for twelve years, was also looking at his laptop. On the screen was a photograph of himself, not exactly smiling, but clearly happy, his mouth open as if making a joyful declaration. Superimposed on the lower portion of the photograph was a text block, in which Ed typed, paused, and typed, formatted, paused, and reformatted. Eventually, Ed sat back, sipping from his cup of still-warm coffee, and read with satisfaction: "At Ed Byrnes and Associates, Words Matter."

*

At Love Field in Dallas, from which the night before the Texas Ranger statue had been removed, Sergeant Clint Peoples said to Officer Charline Jordan, "I looked it up. Lee Roy Young was the first black man allowed to join the Texas Rangers. This was in 1988. That year, only four out of eighty candidates were chosen. I'd bet you a hundred dollars Ranger Young doesn't have any problem with that statue." Officer Jordan asked Sergeant Peoples if he would like her to bring him a bagel, and he said he would appreciate it, paused, and added, "And I appreciate you, Officer Jordan."

*

At the Cook County Jail in Chicago, Celeste's supervisor sat her down at the beginning of a shift in a room similarly furnished as the one in which she had observed The Serial Stowaway during her telephone interview with that reporter. The supervisor told Celeste that she was up for promotion. Celeste shook her head with barely perceptible motion. Thank you, she told her supervisor, but no. Her supervisor asked why. Celeste said she had been with the Department of Corrections for twenty-four years and had been offered promotions before but had always turned them down. "When you don't let them give you anything," she said, "they can't take anything away."

*

At Ben G's Bar in West Dundee, Illinois, Amanda—
O'Hare Airport closed-circuit television monitor by day—
told the owner she had a new comedy set that she thought
people would love, but she had timed it and would need eight
minutes. The owner said she could have the eight minutes if
she would let him fuck her.

"With what?" she said.

One of the regular comedians, a big-bellied man who got
belly laughs telling jokes about his belly, had seen but not
heard the conversation. As Amanda passed, he grabbed her
arm and asked what was up.

She told him that she had a new set but needed more
stage time for it and the owner was being an asshole. The
comedian said he would put in a good word for her if she
would fuck him.

*

Sales were slow for Francis November's book *Love
Yourself and Other Life Lessons of the Glitterati*. Some days,
he placed the blame on his publisher's weak publicity team.
Other days, he thought he should have gone with his alternate title, *7 Habits of Highly Celebrated People*. However, he did
not think about it often. An especially solid streak of celebrity
scandals involving stars he had worked for increased the demand for him as an on-air and online commentator—despite
his assiduous avoidance of spilling any secrets—and that had
helped bring a handful of high-paying coaching clients.

Things were fine. Burn too bright, as he had seen many times in his career, and you burn out. Remember Amy. Remember River. Remember Judy.

*

In Studio D of Platinum Productions, where *D-Listed* was taped, Clarissa Clarke's flamboyant tales of having her identity and room hijacked by The Serial Stowaway so pleased the show's producers that she drew jealous ire from the rest of the cast, the resulting conflict pleasing the producers even more, drawing even more ire from the cast, with the result that, after the show aired, Clarissa was offered a part playing a ditzy celebrity in a credit card commercial, a performance that people enjoyed enough to talk about when not in front of their televisions, rare for a television commercial these days, and to search for old Lewis and Clarke routines on YouTube. Viewers of these routines were disappointed that Clarissa was so under-used in the duo, and went about making popular memes and GIFs from her reaction shots to her partner's wackiness, the latter edited out by this new generation.

*

The shrugging scholar wrote a book manuscript based on his catalogue of shrugging examples. After sixteen months, he received from one publisher a response that offered to consider the manuscript if the author would add a "strong section of concluding comments." The shrugging scholar, without shrugging, responded the same day. "Why should I limit whatever joy you might find from painting your own pictures by painting my own?"

*

The woman who published her journals online stopped doing so. She did not get funding for her startup during the conference in Hawaii nor after that. She retired from social media. She entered a period of life that was quiet and relatively pleasant.

*

The Serial Stowaway's adventure in Los Angeles was her last great public exploit. The news and resulting chatter diminished quickly, and after the coda of news reports about The Serial Stowaway's arrest after a television interview declaring she would never again stow away, silence ensued. For a while, when scrolling through headlines online or turning on news broadcasts, people wondered when they would see another tale of The Serial Stowaway. Occasionally, friends gathering at local coffee shops on Sunday afternoons or people chatting in locker rooms after an exercise session or neighbors sitting in lawn chairs and drinking beer on summer evenings would ask whatever happened to The Serial Stowaway. Once in a while, a lone person sitting on the stool of an anonymous tavern would turn to a stranger several stools

away and, apropos of nothing and not even expecting a response, say, "I remember that lady who stowed away on airplanes." Eventually, even that stopped.

It was at this time of silence when, one Friday in early
April, on the cusp of sunset, a twenty-four-year-old woman
named Bernadette, returning from work in the Chicago
Loop, decided to take a slightly different route for her walk
from the Libertyville Metra station to the house she rented
with two roommates. After two or three blocks on this new
route, plotted by instinct, Bernadette found herself approaching on her right a well-worn three-story apartment
building spread in a three-section arc. Within the arc was
grass of a green surprisingly rich for early spring after a hard
winter and unadorned with trees, shrubs, sculpture, or any
other even modest efforts to create a sense of hominess.

As she drew closer to the building and its blank green
canvas of a lawn, she saw that deep into the space, not far
from the center block of apartments, something white broke
the perfection of the green. Now standing on the sidewalk at
the midpoint of the lawn, directly opposite the center block
of the building, she recognized the white on the grass as a
piece of rope. It appeared to be cotton, the weight of rope
that would be used to hang wash across a courtyard. Bernadette guessed its length at about four feet, although this was
hard to judge accurately because the rope lay in irregular
curves and loops.

Wondering, casually, why a piece of litter would be allowed to linger on such an otherwise neat lawn, Bernadette
continued, enjoying the novelty of her new route home.

Saturday was a busy day for Bernadette, but Sunday, while one load of laundry was in the basement washer and another in the dryer, feeling the allure of bright sun and fresh air, she decided to take a short walk.

Without much thought, she found herself again on Library Lane and soon nearing the apartment house with the neat green lawn. Recalling her Friday afternoon sighting, she glanced toward the lawn and saw a line of white still there, still breaking up the plane of green. As she closed in on the building, she saw that it was the same type of rope, same weight, same color, but it was also different. It seemed to be lying in a different position, to describe a different shape. Bernadette was not sure, but she thought that on Friday afternoon the rope had a broad loop on one side, and now the rope was more elongated—curved, but with no loops. Well, she thought, some kid probably picked it up and dropped it again.

She pulled her phone from her back pocket, touched the camera icon, and took a picture of the rope.

On Monday, morning and afternoon, Bernadette took her usual route to and from the train station, but on Tuesday, feeling angry at her boss for no particular reason, desiring even a small gesture of independence, she diverted from her usual route and again found herself on Library Lane approaching the three-story apartment building. She had taken a later train, and the sun had just passed the horizon, but the white line on the green lawn, although not as striking in the fading light, was still visible.

Bernadette made for the position opposite the building

and surprised herself by setting her shoulder bag on the side-walk, which seemed to indicate she would be there for a while. Leaving her bag behind—it contained her work-issued laptop, and she thought perhaps she would be lucky and someone would steal it—she stepped onto the lawn and to-ward the piece of rope.

It may have been the same piece of rope, or maybe it wasn't, but she was certain it was in a different shape. Just to be sure, she took her phone from her back pocket and com-pared today's position with Sunday's photograph. Yes, dif-ferent. Two loops and the rope lay more diagonally than hor-izontally in relationship to the building. She thought it looked like the rope was getting ready to tie itself into a bow. She took a photograph of the rope and turned, feeling disap-pointed when she saw that her shoulder bag still rested on the sidewalk.

Although fairly regular in her habits, Bernadette was pulled one way and another by friends, work, and life's re-sponsibilities, while in turn she pushed with her own projects and sporadic endeavors. Thus, she did not pass the apart-ment building and its green lawn every day, but she made a point of passing it several times a week. Each time, the rope was there. Each time, it described a different shape. Each time, she took a photograph.

Bernadette's office was what is called an open environ-ment, which meant she sat in a big room, her laptop between other laptops on one of the narrow surfaces that stretched the width of the room. These surfaces faced chest-high ledges, on the other side of which were other long surfaces with other people on laptops facing those across the ledge. Every telephone conversation, every bit of chatter, and every oath muttered at a laptop screen was more or less audible. She could and did wear earbuds to block out the sound, but the louder sounds penetrated, and even the less loud sounds were still a perceptible murmur. And of course, the earbuds did nothing to block out the endless random motion of people in her peripheral vision. No workspaces were assigned, and even if they had been, the layout all but precluded personal items such as framed photographs of family members.

In this setting of depersonalization masquerading as collaboration, Bernadette thought she saw an opportunity. The ledges dividing the rows of people at their laptops were rarely used. They were just a bit too high and just a bit too distant to be a convenient place to put any paper related to the project at hand, and in any case, paper was not used much in this workplace.

Bernadette bought a device designed to print at small size photographs from one's phone. At home, she printed photographs of the rope, which she brought to work and arranged on whichever ledge happened to abut whichever workstation she occupied, replacing them each day with other photographs of the rope on that day's ledge at that day's workstation. Coworkers would pause in such a way that made it clear they saw the photographs, but never commented. Eventually, Bernadette stopped bringing the photographs to work, feeling, in some way she could not articulate, that the effort was a failure.

She did, however, find herself, while facing a spreadsheet

or a PowerPoint slide or a gallery of people on a video call on her screen, thinking about the rope.

She thought about the rope's shapes. Sometimes the rope looked like a hand reaching out, sometimes like the outline of a storybook house, sometimes like a train engine, sometimes like a dancer extending a leg preparatory to running.

She thought about how the rope mingled with its environment. On rainy days, the rope absorbed the moisture in ways that gave its surface new dimension, which she attempted to capture with more tightly framed photographs. When the first snow fell, the white rope seemed to be hiding, evoking a sense of hibernation appropriate for the season.

She thought about where the rope came from. At first, she thought someone might be accidentally dropping the rope as part of some task related to the apartment building, but she couldn't imagine what sort of task would generate that sort of output. She wondered if someone each day carefully laid the rope at this spot in a new shape, but the shapes seemed too random, too inadvertent to be the product of human decision. She wondered if someone walked past the spot each day and dropped the rope, but once the snowfall started, she saw no footprints leading to or from the spot where the rope lay each day.

That all but confirmed the rope was being dropped from above. Once Bernadette ruled out helicopters and drones—as pleasant as it was to imagine these as means of rope-dropping—she could only conclude that someone was dropping the rope each day from an apartment window, one of the apartments in the row directly above the spot where the rope lay.

The first-floor apartment, she decided, was the least likely. Although the rope lay in roughly the same spot each day, the spot had enough variation to suggest that air currents were at work influencing where the rope landed. The second-floor apartment was even less likely because in the window that overlooked the spot was a sign for a losing candidate in an election that had been held three years previously, and Bernadette could hardly imagine the person who lived there would, each day, move the sign to allow for tossing a rope out the window and then replace the sign.

The third-floor apartment it was. While at work, Bernadette would visualize the person who lived in this apartment. She researched the building and discovered it was low-income housing for people fifty-five and older. So, the person was not a young, clove-cigarette-smoking conceptual artist. The person was probably unemployed or retired, gray-haired or white-haired. The person was, she hoped, a woman. How would she be dressed? Bernadette struggled to imagine. What expression was on the face of the occupant of this apartment when she made each day's rope drop? Mischievous? Furtive? Matter of fact? Neutral? Was the rope-drop the highlight of her day, or something she did between drinking a cup of tea and showering, something done while thinking about something entirely different or about nothing at all? Did she look out the window at the shape that resulted? Or was the act of dropping the rope satisfying in itself?

Bernadette began to dawdle when passing the apartment

building on foot, staring up at the third-floor window for any sign of movement. She eyed anyone who happened to enter or leave the building's main door when she passed, trying to picture the person at the window, piece of rope in hand. She passed the apartment at different times of the day, particularly on mornings, trying to catch the rope-dropper in the act.

Once, on a drizzling day, hood over her head and drooping into her field of vision, Bernadette was certain she saw a curtain being pulled to one side in the window. What she saw in the gap she was less certain. It may have been real, or it may have been some combination of the drizzle, the hood, and the desire for some result from her search. But what Bernadette thought she saw was this: a slender figure who, perhaps, just perhaps, was giving a faint finger-wave of greeting.

It was inevitable that, as other interests entered Bernadette's life, she would visit the apartment building less frequently. Sometimes when she did pass, she neglected to photograph the rope, although it was always there in whatever shape the vicissitudes of gravity, air currents, aerodynamics, and chance had produced that day.

Bernadette got a new job, in an office in which she had a dedicated cubicle, in another suburb more conveniently reached by car than train, so she no longer walked past the apartment building to and from the Metra station, and she was in too much of a hurry to get to work to detour past the apartment building, and she was too preoccupied reviewing the novel events of these novel days to pass it in the evening.

Eventually, Bernadette moved to another city and had an office with walls and a door. Bernadette became less young and then not young. She still thought about the rope and about the woman she may or may not have seen through the window. She thought it might be a good story for a party, but she could never quite figure out a way to tell it that would result in something other than blank stares or bemusement.

Mostly, when Bernadette thought about the rope in the grass, the apartment, the window, and the wave, she did so on late afternoons in early April, just before dusk, on days much like the day when she first saw the vague shape of the randomly placed rope on the perfectly green grass.

ABOUT THE AUTHOR

Robert Fromberg wrote the award-winning memoir *How to Walk with Steve* (Latah Books), the historical novel *Gee, That Was Fun: 7 Days of Mayhem, 1983* (Trunk of My Car Cooperative), the collection of essays and stories *Friends and Fiends, Pulp Stars and Pop Stars* (Alien Buddha Press), and the novella *Blue Skies* (Floating Island Publications). He taught writing for many years at Northwestern University and lives in Madison, Wisconsin.

More information: robertfromberg.com.